m
not very
good

R

D1575341

HER GOOD THING

This Large Print Book carries the
Seal of Approval of N.A.V.H.

HER GOOD THING

VANESSA MILLER

THORNDIKE PRESS
A part of Gale, Cengage Learning

GALE
CENGAGE Learning

Detroit • New York • San Francisco • New Haven, Conn • Waterville, Maine • London

GALE
CENGAGE Learning·

Copyright © 2012 by Vanessa Miller.
Thorndike Press, a part of Gale, Cengage Learning.

LIBRARY OF CONGRESS CATALOGING-IN-PUBLICATION DATA

Miller, Vanessa.
  Her Good Thing / by Vanessa Miller. — Large Print edition.
    pages cm. — (Thorndike Press Large Print African-American)
  ISBN-13: 978-1-4104-5616-8 (hardcover)
  ISBN-10: 1-4104-5616-1 (hardcover)
  1. African American women—Fiction. 2. Advertising agencies—Texas—Houston—Fiction. 3. Houston (Tex.)—Fiction. 4. Large type books. I. Title.
  PS3613.I5623H47 2013
  813'.6—dc23   2012044695

Published in 2013 by arrangement with Harlequin Books S.A.

Printed in Mexico
1 2 3 4 5 6 7 17 16 15 14 13

To my grandson, Jarod Harris, for all the joy you bring into my life.

Dear Reader,

The idea for *Her Good Thing* comes from a Bible verse that says, "The man who finds a wife finds a good thing and obtains favor from the Lord."

Well, I thought it would be fun to turn that verse upside down and have the woman try to find her good thing, rather than wait on the man to find her. But the truth is, Danetta Harris's good thing has always been there, in the gorgeous form of her best friend and business partner, Marshall Windham.

Danetta has been in love with Marshall for years, but has finally given up all fantasies of the two of them walking down the aisle together. As Danetta starts looking for love in all the wrong places, Marshall begins to see what has been staring him in the face all along. But has he waited too long?

Her Good Thing is a part of a three-book series titled For Your Love, and it's all about women going after their men. In the process they run into some funny situations that will make you laugh, but they also deal with a few gut-wrenching situations that just might bring a tear to your eye. I hope you will enjoy the stories of love, loss and adventure that the three women of the For Your Love series bring to life.

As you read this series I'd love to hear from you. Email me at vmiller-01@earthlink.net so we can chat about Danetta, Ryla and Surry.

Happy reading,
Vanessa Miller

CHAPTER 1

"We women are born nurturers," said the speaker. "We tend to let the men in our lives take center stage while we stand behind them, doing all the work."

Danetta Harris rolled her eyes as she received yet another urgent message from Marshall Windham, her business partner, and the poster boy for the message the speaker was delivering to the Women's Empowerment group at that very moment. Marshall invaded Danetta's dreams and he consumed her thoughts when she should have been concentrating on far more important matters. Because Marshall Windham was all wrong for her. The man had a brilliant mind for business and was Idris Elba fine. Not the Idris Elba who worked in a mechanic shop in *Daddy's Little Girls* but the Idris Elba who was so fine in those gray pants with the black button-down shirt who strutted away from an exploding airplane in

Takers. And that was the problem. Marshall was a taker and an unreformed ladies' man.

The speaker said, "It's time to enact your Get Success Now plan and get on with creating the life you were born to live."

Another text from Marshall came in. Why haven't you called me? I need you.

Danetta stood up and walked out from the back of the conference room. She sat down at a table near the bookstore and called Marshall. *He thinks he can bug me at any hour of the day or night,* she huffed. She understood that they ran a business together and therefore needed to make themselves available, but it was eight o'clock on a Friday night. *What could be so urgent?*

"Hey, where are you?" Marshall asked the moment he answered his phone.

"I'm at the symposium I told you about," Danetta said, trying to keep the irritation out of her voice. "Why? What's up?"

Marshall's hearty laugh crossed the phone line and pierced Danetta's heart. "That's why you're still single. I mean, really, Danetta, you take that I-am-woman-hear-me-roar stuff a bit too far and it is a major turnoff to most of the men I know."

Most of the men he knew were Snoop Doggie-dogs. "Your text said urgent. So, what do you want?"

"Hey, no need to get your back up. I'm just looking out for your best interests. You're not getting any younger."

That stung. "Look, Marshall, I know you haven't been blowing up my phone all evening just so we could talk about my love life. Now tell me what you want or I'm hanging up."

"I'm packing for the retreat and I was hoping that you had changed your mind about attending it with me."

The man was impossible. She had signed Marshall up for a business retreat that was notorious for being a "boy's club" event. A few women attended, but unless they were multimillionaire businesswomen like the current CEO of Hewlett-Packard, Meg Whitman, or the former CEO Carly Fiorina, they were pretty much ignored. Danetta wasn't worried; women had business retreats all the time. All Danetta wanted was the business that these companies could bring to their firm . . . and all Marshall wanted was someone else to do the networking for him. "I can't help you mingle and network this time, Marshall. This is a men's thing, remember?"

Born with clout and money, Marshall was in his element around presidents and CEOs. He simply hated networking. He said it just seemed too much like begging to him and Marshall didn't beg anyone for anything. "We both know why you're not going, Danetta, and it has nothing to do with how many men attend the retreat."

He was right. There had been countless times when they'd received invitations that were clearly meant for the head man in charge. Danetta would go anyway; she loved showing those self-important men that her pants fit just as well as theirs. But she also preferred to drive to the events.

"Why don't you just get over your fear of flying and join me at this event?"

"I don't have a fear of flying."

"Then what is it, D, because I'd really like to have you with me this weekend." The conference Marshall was attending was in New York and the flight from Houston, Texas, where they lived was just too long for her to stomach.

"I am not about to trust some pilot with my life just so you don't have to mix and mingle."

"The mix and mingle I have no problem with. I'm just not as good at asking for business as you are. And since when do you trust anybody with your life, let alone a pilot?"

Danetta gave a heavy sigh. "Drop it, Marshall."

"All right D, if you're dead set against going, then maybe I should take a date with me." It was a tease. They had already discussed why he shouldn't take a date.

"I explained to you why that was a bad idea," she reminded him through gritted teeth

"Yeah, but when I told Veronica she couldn't go, she broke up with me."

"Why would she do that?"

"Because she thinks I'm taking another woman."

Marshall was talking, but all Danetta heard was *ruff-ruff-ruff*. He was a dog and she was a fool. She couldn't believe that she had wasted years of her life waiting for this man to change his ways so that they could finally be together. But she was done hoping and wishing for this man who treated women like accessories . . . picking whichever one matched his mood for the day. She didn't even know who Veronica was. The last she knew, Marshall was dating a woman named Diane. "In case you forgot, the last woman you took on a business outing got drunk and threw up on our client."

He chuckled. "Yeah, but she apologized."

She threw up her hands. "Do what you

want, Marshall, but if you make a fool of yourself this weekend, you'll be looking for another business partner next week."

"Calm down, Danetta. I'll go alone."

"Thank you," Danetta said, and then hung up. She was about ready to go tickety-boom. And if the truth was told, she didn't want to go back into that conference room to hear the speaker pronounce her a fool for desiring a man who wanted nothing to do with her. Yet, she had put her career in his hands. She would have left the meeting and gone home much sooner because her conversation with Marshall had drained all of her energy, but she had given her two best friends, Surry McDaniel and Ryla Evans, a ride. She couldn't just abandon them, no matter that she was to the point of foaming at the mouth.

Why had she gone into business with Marshall Windham in the first place? *Because he's gorgeous and brilliant and you fell in love with him from the moment he walked into your art class at Howard University,* Danetta reminded herself.

Okay, Danetta confessed, *I might have been a real good Boo-Boo-the-Fool for Marshall, but even fools stop falling and bumping their heads at some point.* Danetta had finally come to terms with the fact that

Marshall would never stop chasing after women long enough to notice her.

"Girl, what has gotten into you?" Surry asked, as she and Ryla came out of the conference room and sat down next to Danetta.

"You missed the best part of her speech," Ryla said, sitting down on the opposite side of Danetta.

Danetta smiled as her girls sat down with her. On the surface it appeared that Surry, Ryla and Danetta didn't have enough in common to be as tight as they were. Surry thought that straightening combs were evil and that the relaxer was a diabolical invention by Satan, designed to damage the hair of every black woman in America. Surry wore her hair in an afro or braids, and her wardrobe was strictly Afrocentric. Ryla on the other hand wouldn't walk to her mailbox without a fresh relaxer and a cute hair cut. Ryla was a stylish former beauty queen, prom queen and cheerleader, while Danetta was all business with eyeglasses, knee- or calf-length skirts and turtleneck sweaters.

"And why did you keep checking your cell phone? You normally turn that thing off. What if you were giving the presentation? You wouldn't want people in the audience sending text messages and ignoring you al-

15

together," Ryla said.

They were right. This wasn't the first time Marshall had sent her numerous text messages during a business meeting, lunch with friends or even when she was having dinner with Aunt Sarah. As a matter of fact, Marshall often wrangled an invitation to dinner from Aunt Sarah, so he didn't have to interrupt her during dinner, because he was there, eating it with them.

At that moment she realized that she had made herself too accessible to Marshall, and she was tired of living on his terms.

"Well, I may have walked out early, but I think she said the most important thing before I left."

"And what was that?" Surry asked.

"That we as women need to enact our success plan."

"What are you talking about, Danetta? You're already successful. After all, you are co-owner of a multimillion dollar advertising firm," Ryla reminded her.

"I'm not talking about business success. I guess I'm just fed up with being single and feel that it's time to enact my Get Love Now plan," Danetta said with conviction in her voice.

"What did that mongrel do now?" Ryla asked, as she rolled her eyes heavenward.

From the moment Danetta had first spilled her guts about Marshall, Ryla had dubbed him a mongrel. She'd said that he was half human and half dog. Danetta had laughed at the time, but the way she was feeling today, Danetta wondered if Ryla was being too generous. As far as she was concerned, Marshall was a full-bred hound dog.

"Why would my discontent have anything to do with Marshall Windham?"

"Well, let's see," Surry pretended to be thinking. "You have been in love with the man for over a decade, and you bake up a dozen brownies and eat them with a bucketful of vanilla ice cream each time Marshall starts dating someone new," Surry answered.

"I'm done with all of that." Danetta stood up and grabbed her purse. "Come on. I'm going to take you two home, so I can get started on making new plans for my life."

Ryla harrumphed. "You can't plan out every detail of your life, Danetta. Some things just happen and there's nothing you can do about it." Ryla had learned that simple fact all too well. She was a twenty-eight-year-old single mother of an adorable seven-year-old princess.

"I planned out my business life, and if I

17

do say so myself, I have become quite successful." Danetta put her key in the ignition and started the car the moment Ryla and Surry closed their doors. As she drove out of the parking lot, she said, "What hasn't been going so well is my love life, and that's because I've been too busy with business and hanging with a bunch of women —"

"Hey," Ryla protested.

"— to develop a meaningful relationship with a man," Danetta finished.

"Well, excuse us for inhaling the same air as you," Surry said from the backseat.

"I know you're not objecting to my wanting to find a man, Surry. You seem to have a new man every week."

"That's because I haven't met one that I wanted to keep yet." Surry corrected Danetta, "And it's not every week . . . maybe every other week."

"I've met some of the men you've dated. They seemed perfectly fine to me," Danetta challenged.

"That's until you dig a little deeper," Surry said. "None of them are serious about righting the wrongs of blacks and most don't even know who Marcus Garvey was. And what has really ticked me off lately with some of these so-called brothers is that most of them wanted to take me out, but didn't want to help me canvas the streets for President Obama's reelection campaign."

"Don't expect any tears from me. These men drool all over you, like you're their Nubian queen and all you do is toss them aside." *And who could blame them,* Danetta thought, *even with all her eccentric behavior, Surry can't hide the fact that she looks like the supermodel, Iman.*

"Yeah, Surry, don't expect us to feel sorry for you," Ryla chimed in. "I can't date because of all the mess I'm already in with my child who has never seen her father. So, I'm not trying to go down that road again."

"And whose fault is that? You're the one who left that man without so much as a word about your pregnancy," Surry answered back.

"Okay," Danetta held up a hand. "Let's not get started on a subject that will take us someplace we don't want to be."

The three women agreed and then continued discussing Danetta's Get Love Now plan. By the time she had dropped her friends off, she had pretty much convinced herself that a change of plans was exactly what she needed.

She stopped off at the bakery around the corner from her house and purchased two brownies. *Yeah, yeah,* Danetta mused, *Mar-*

shall starting up with this Veronica chick does bother me, but I'm not going to spend an entire week eating a whole pan of brownies and a tub of ice cream. I'll drown my sorrows tonight, but tomorrow I'll learn to swim in a new pond.

CHAPTER 2

Yawning and stretching, Marshall eased himself into a sitting position. With his back against the headboard of his king-size bed, he rubbed his eyes as he looked at the clock on his nightstand. It was six in the morning and the doorbell was ringing. Reluctantly, he got out of bed and made his way to the front door. He unlocked the door and then opened it. He was surprised to see Veronica standing on his porch holding a small suitcase.

"I'm here," she said with a bright and cheery smile on her face. "I'm ready to go."

With her hair pulled back into a ponytail, Veronica looked more like Danetta than he'd noticed when they'd first met. Danetta, however, would never have just shown up on his doorstep after he'd already informed her that she would not be taking this trip with him. At that moment, Marshall felt the need to remind Veronica that they were no longer dating. "You do remember that you broke up with me, right?"

"I was just mad that you tried to cancel our trip, but I'm over all that now."

She looked so cute with her honey-blond hair pulled back that he wanted to ignore Danetta's request, get his overnight bag and ride out of town with Veronica. Danetta just didn't believe in having fun anymore. But whether Danetta knew how to have fun or not wasn't the issue. Marshall had promised her that he wouldn't mess things up for their company, and he planned to keep his word. "Sorry, hon, I can't take you on this trip."

Veronica's smile disappeared as she snarled, "You jerk. So, it's like Diane said, huh? You really are going to take her on this trip instead of me."

"Diane is just messing with your head. Now I'm sorry, but I've got to go, Veronica." He closed the front door and headed back toward his bedroom. Two weeks after he and Diane had called their relationship quits, Marshall had accepted a dinner invitation from Veronica. Diane had gotten so upset that she'd been lying to her about him ever since. He'd unknowingly dated a pair of friends back when he was in high school, and it had ended badly: with the air being let out of his tires.

He would have taken the time to explain things a little more to Veronica and would have even let her in on the situation with the retreat, but Marshall was offended that Veronica would accuse him of two-timing her with Diane. He might date a lot of women, but Marshall had this rule to only date one woman at a time. And he never went back for seconds. Once he was done with a woman, that was it. As a matter of fact, he didn't even like the idea of dating friends; that high school incident had taught him well. The only reason he'd even considered dating Veronica was because she looked so much like Danetta, but he probably needed therapy to uncover why that even made a difference to him. He went into the bathroom off his master bedroom, turned on the shower and got in. As the hot water steamed up the room, Marshall's thoughts drifted to Danetta Harris, the only woman, besides his mama, that he'd managed to have a decent relationship with for over a decade. She was his buddy, his comrade. Their friendship had even survived a seven-year business partnership.

Marshall had been a junior and she had been in the second semester of her freshman year when they'd met. He'd thought she was one of the prettiest girls on campus. Not beautiful, but pretty and wholesome . . . the kind of girl his mother would have begged him to marry. That was the reason he'd kept Danetta in the friend zone. He had been too young to fall in love, and had no clue how to keep a woman like Danetta happy. So when Danetta had come to him one night after finals and confessed that she wanted to hook up with him, Marshall had told her that he liked her much better as a friend and didn't want anything to spoil their friendship . . . like a marriage, three kids and a nasty divorce.

Even after that awkward evening, Danetta had stuck by him. Whatever he needed, she had always been there for him. And in return he'd made her a full partner in the company he founded. When he'd offered her the job, Marshall had told Danetta that he needed her to help him conquer the world. He didn't know why he felt that way, but it was true. With Danetta as COO of Windham Enterprises, the company had tripled its profits within three years. As far as Marshall was concerned, he'd made a good call when he chose Danetta as a friend.

Slam . . . bang . . . boom!

"What the devil?" Marshall heard a loud crashing sound coming from his bedroom.

He turned off the shower, put a towel around his waist and then opened his bathroom door. The first thing he noticed as he stepped into his bedroom was that his mirror had been shattered and the ceramic lamp Danetta had bought him for his thirtieth birthday was broken into hundreds of pieces and now lay in the middle of his floor. "Are you crazy?" he asked Veronica. "How did you get into my house?"

"Shouldn't leave your door unlocked when you're trying to be a player." Her eyes darted wildly around the room as she looked for something else to throw.

"How am I playing you?" He was perplexed. He thought he was perfectly clear with her. "What are you talking about?"

"I just called Diane and she said that she was packed and waiting for you."

He held up his hands in frustration. "She's lying. If I had wanted Diane, I would have never started seeing you." Marshall had dated Diane for about two months and then Veronica for three . . . about a month longer than he should have. But he enjoyed companionship on his business trips, and Veronica had been fun to hang out with. So, he'd kept the relationship going a little longer than he should have.

"Yeah, right. Then why aren't you taking

me to this retreat?"

As far as Marshall was concerned, Danetta look-alike or not, he would never take this woman anywhere again. But she had that mad-black-woman look in her eyes, so he wasn't about to let her in on his little secret. He just wanted to keep the peace, and get her out of his house. "It's business, Veronica. That's why I'm not taking you. There's no other reason."

She picked up one of his Italian leather shoes and threw it at his head. "You've taken me on business trips before," she said, as she ran out of the bedroom.

He ducked like former President Bush and then, Marshall thought about running after Veronica, but he needed to figure out how to maneuver his way around the room without getting broken glass in his feet. He jumped on his bed and then climbed down on the opposite side of the room. He really didn't want to go after Veronica. The only reason he was even attempting to find her was in case she was in his kitchen grabbing a butcher knife. He'd seen *Fatal Attraction* and all those other some-man-did-me-wrong-and-I-done-lost-my-mind movies. "Veronica, where are you?"

She didn't answer, but he heard footsteps that were headed toward his living room.

He just hoped that she didn't decide to break up any of the valuable antiques in that room. Most of the antiques and portraits in his living room had been purchased during trips outside the country. So, it wasn't as if he could just run over to Italy or England and replace the stuff. "You've got it all wrong, Veronica. I'm not taking you to the retreat because my business partner doesn't think it's a good idea. I'm not taking anyone else either." He tried to smooth things over before *his* mad black woman went Madea on him . . . found his electric saw and then cut his leather couch in half. Even though the guy in that movie was completely wrong for the way he'd treated his wife, Marshall had still cringed when Tyler Perry's Madea had started tearing up the house. No man wants the stuff he's worked hard for to get torn up. And every guy he knew could think of at least one woman with reason enough to tear his stuff up.

"Liar," she screamed as she opened the front door and slammed it behind her.

Marshall pumped his fist in the air. "Yes!" he said, as he heard the door slam. But he wasn't taking any chances. He rushed over to the front door and locked it before going back to his bedroom. He grabbed his cell phone off the nightstand and called his cleaning lady. She agreed to come back to the house and take care of the bedroom. He then threw on some clothes, pulled his overnight bag out of the closet and grabbed his keys. When he stepped outside and saw the key marks on his midnight black Cadillac SUV, he simply shook his head. This wasn't his first time dealing with a woman who couldn't handle the end of a relationship, but he hadn't gone through this kind of drama since his late twenties. At thirty-two, dealing with a scorned woman was getting a bit old.

Danetta had done five miles on her treadmill. Two was the most she normally did in the morning, but after eating both of those brownies and half of her bucket of ice cream last night, she figured she needed those extra miles. She towel dried her face and neck as she stepped off the treadmill, and then walked upstairs to her home office.

On Saturday mornings she normally kicked back and tried to relax after her workout but she had work to do today. Today's work had nothing to do with the advertising agency. Although, maybe some of the skills she'd acquired as an advertising executive could help her out with her manhunt. After all, she was skilled in product placement and creative design. Some of her knowledge would come in handy for the task at hand.

Opening her file cabinet, Danetta searched for the file labeled Husband Material. As she pulled it out, a picture of her and Marshall tumbled out and fell to the floor. As she bent down to pick it up, a smile crept across her honey-toned face. They had been hugging as they sat on the steps that led to the Howard University student library and a friend had snapped a picture of them. Danetta's head lay on Marshall's chest, while he put his arms around her and drew her closer to him. Danetta had hoped that Marshall would open his eyes and see her as more than a friend. But the night she threw herself at him, he'd made it abundantly clear that he was just not that into her.

Humiliated after that crushing blow to her self-esteem, Danetta had gone from one man's bed to the next, trying to take back her heart. But none of the men she'd dated had measured up to Marshall Windham, and her heart remained broken. So, she finally stopped trying to date and just concentrated on her career.

And now she needed to move on with her life. She opened the file and began reading the list she had created about five years ago that detailed her perfect man. At the top of her list was the fact that she wanted to spend her life with a man that she could trust with her heart.

"So why'd you keep this picture of Marshall inside your Husband Material file?" she wondered out loud. Marshall was his own number-one fan and couldn't possibly do right by her. But as she read the rest of the list and was reminded that she wanted a man who would be about his business, charming, handsome, adventurous, financially secure and someone who was able to make her smile . . . who enjoyed the same things she did, she realized that Marshall fit every characteristic but the first one.

Then Danetta got to thinking about where she had gone wrong. She reasoned that no one was perfect, and if she continued to wait for a man who satisfied her every hope and dream, she might be alone for a long time to come. But what if she threw away her list and just began to date men whom she found interesting. She jotted "lose the list" on the notepad on her desk.

She stood up and began pacing the floor. "Okay, I can forget about everything but my number-one item. I have to be able to trust the man I marry . . . bottom line."

She walked into her bedroom and stood in front of the full-length mirror. Danetta knew she wasn't beautiful or what men would consider sensual or alluring by any means. She had long hair that she mostly put into a ponytail or in a tight bun atop her head. It was just too much trouble and too time consuming to worry about styling her hair every morning. Since she had just finished her morning workout, Danetta was wearing a jogging suit, but her normal attire was business casual with an emphasis on below the knee or calf-length skirts or loose-fitting navy blue, black or brown pants.

Her face was devoid of makeup. In fact, Danetta rarely wore anything more than her favorite Crème d' Nude lipstick from M.A.C. and a little mascara. She'd never understood how or why women took the time to put all that war paint on their faces, when they would just have to wash it all off later that evening.

The longer she checked out her image in the mirror, the more confused she became. Danetta had no clue what men were looking for in a woman. It had simply been too long since her last date. She needed help from an expert.

Her phone rang. She saw that it was Marshall so she picked it up. "Hey, whatcha doing?" he asked.

Danetta grabbed the remote and hurriedly turned on her television. "Nothing much, just watching TV."

"Whatcha watching?"

She hit the guide to see what channel her TV was on. "The Hallmark Channel."

"One of those love movies, huh?"

"What if it is?" Rolling her eyes, even though Marshall had watched these movies with her on more than one occasion, he thought the whole thing was a joke and that the kind of love they showed on television didn't really exist. Although she could swear that she heard him sniffling during *An Affair to Remember.*

"Don't get testy. I was just asking. Which one is on today?"

"It's called *Love Begins.* I read the book. It was written by Janette Oke."

"So, why watch the movie if you know how it ends?" Marshall asked.

Irritated by the question, especially since she was only pretending to watch the movie, she said, "Was there a reason for your call?"

"I always call you when I'm out of town . . . well, unless I'm having a real good time."

"Yeah, I know all about your *real* good times. Look, I've got to go."

"All right . . . I was just checking on you."

Danetta wanted desperately to ask him how a woman would go about finding a man, but she was too embarrassed to let Marshall know that she had lost her groove on the dating tip, so she just hung up and called Ryla.

Her best friend was not only beautiful and savvy when it came to business matters, but she knew how to handle men. Lately, all Ryla did was turn men down, but she even did that with panache. Danetta picked up the phone and dialed her friend's number. When Ryla answered, she said, "I need your help."

"What's up, girl? I was just about to take Jaylen to her ballet class."

Danetta took a deep breath and rushed out her request. "I need to know how to get men interested in me."

"What . . . What did you say?"

"You heard me. I told you last night that I was going to adjust my plans. And my new strategy is to go on as many dates as possible. But I have to get someone to ask me out first, and I need help with that."

"It sounds like you need Surry; she's the serial dater."

"Yeah, but I'd never get away with wearing some of the outfits she puts on. And besides, I need help finding a man to settle down with. Surry isn't interested in that."

"Wow," was all Ryla could say.

"Stop acting as if this is some big deal. I just need to figure out how to get men interested in me."

"I've known you for five years, and you've never gone after men. I mean, you've seen Marshall naked, and you can't even look him in the eye and tell him how you feel."

"I've only seen Marshall's bare chest, and that's it. And anyway, this has nothing to do with Marshall." Danetta nearly screamed those words at the top of her lungs.

"Don't kid yourself, Danetta. Everything you do has something to do with that mongrel boy."

"Okay, well let's just say that what I'm doing now is about moving on with my life and finding someone who wants to be a part of it."

"I've never seen you bat one eyelash in another man's direction. So, are you really telling me that you are now ready to go find you a man?"

Ryla had a point. Danetta was definitely stepping outside of her comfort zone. She'd always been shy when it came to the opposite sex. Especially after being shot down by Marshall, Danetta made sure to never approach a man . . . every date she'd been on, the man had asked her out. And that was the problem, because no man had asked in quite some time. "That's why I need you, girl. You know how to flirt. You know how to attract a man's attention. I haven't tried to do anything like that in so long that if I started winking and blinking, the guy would probably think I had a nervous tick or something."

Ryla laughed. "Girl, shut up. Okay, if this is what you really want to do, I'll help you. Matter of fact, meet me at Adorable Hair and Nails at one o'clock this afternoon."

"What's going on there?"

"I have a hair appointment, but I'm going to reschedule with Marlene and ask her to do you up instead." Ryla sounded excited.

Danetta frowned. "I don't know if I need to spend all that time in a hair salon. I was thinking that you could help me put a few outfits together. I have tons of clothes, but I don't think I'm wearing them in a manner that will attract men."

"You can say that again, Ms. Baggy Pants. And just the fact that you don't understand the value of pampering yourself at a hair salon lets me know that I need to be charging for my services 'cause this is going to take a while."

CHAPTER 3

Marshall ran into another scorned woman during the retreat. He'd been having lunch with a couple of Fortune 500 CEOs, regaling them with tales of his college misdeeds, when someone tapped him on the shoulder. He turned in his seat and immediately plastered a smile on his face as he stared at the mocha-chocolate beauty in front of him. "Well hello," Marshall said, thinking that his weekend retreat just got a bit more interesting.

"Hello, Marshall, it's been quite a while," the woman said.

Her voice was so sexy that all conversation stopped at his table as the other men turned and stared. Marshall was flattered that out of all the powerful men in the room, this chocolate goddess chose him. But she spoke his name with familiarity, and he honestly didn't remember her.

At his silence, she continued to speak.

"You don't know who I am, do you?"

"I'd like to know." He turned back to the men at the table and said, "Would you all excuse me for a minute?" He stood up, placed his hand on the woman's back and walked toward the lobby with her. "So, would you like to tell me where we met?"

She sat down on the couch in the lobby, ran her hands through her long coal-black hair and waited for Marshall to sit down next to her. "You really don't remember, do you?"

He wished that he could tell this woman that he not only remembered their meeting, but he'd kept the memory of her close to his heart. But he got nothing when he looked into her face. He met beautiful women all the time. He shook his head in defeat.

"Five years ago I met you at a conference just like this one. You took me out to dinner, whispered in my ear and then we went to your hotel room and you made love to me. I wouldn't normally consider a one-night affair to be lovemaking, but I honestly thought we had connected in a special way."

Marshall wanted to rub his hands together in sweet anticipation. He was about to get his freak on. He was about to ask if she wanted to go to his hotel room now and share a little afternoon delight with him, but she interrupted his thoughts.

"At least I thought we had a special connection. But after waiting by the phone for the call you promised to make, a call that never came, I realized that you don't have a heart. And you had only been playing with mine."

"Now wait a minute. You're trying to make me out to be the bad guy, but if you just met me that weekend and went to bed with me, then you knew what time it was," he argued.

Her voice rose. "You promised to call me."

Marshall shrugged. He couldn't understand what the big deal was. Five years ago his motto had been "love 'em and leave 'em, no strings attached". And he made sure every woman he got involved with understood that. If this woman hadn't received the memo, he didn't know what to tell her.

Fire flared in her eyes as she stood up. "You're so smug and confident. It probably doesn't bother you at all that I dreamed about you that night."

He leaned back and stuck his chest out. "Thank you," he said with a smile that said, *oh yeah, I'm the man.*

She smacked him.

That took the smile off his face, but he

didn't retaliate. He didn't believe that a man should hit a woman under any circumstance, but Veronica and this woman right here were seriously trying his patience.

"One day some woman is going to break your heart. She's going to use you, and then discard you as if you're nothing. After that, maybe you'll finally be housebroken." And with those lovely words she turned and strutted off.

The thing Danetta loved most about Houston was the subtropical weather. They were ten days into February and it was sixty-one degrees. As Danetta got out of the car at Adorable Hair and Nails, she left her jacket in the car and allowed the cool breeze to move her forward. Ryla, Marlene and a few other workers in the salon were standing outside holding balloons in their hands. As she approached, they each let go of the strings, and the balloons floated heavenward. "What's up with the balloons?"

"Girl, we are celebrating the end of that tired ponytail you wear almost every single day," Ryla said.

"Whatever," Danetta said, as she walked into the salon. "I like my ponytail. It's quick and easy."

"And unattractive," Marlene countered.

"Did I come here to be insulted or to get my hair done?" Danetta asked.

"Girl, just sit yourself in Marlene's chair so we can tell you how this is going to go," Ryla said, as she grabbed Danetta's arm and guided her to the shop chair.

Danetta sat down. "Now what do you have up your sleeve?"

Ryla grinned as she looked at Marlene and then back to Danetta. "Here's the deal. I'm paying, so I don't want to hear any complaints."

Danetta shook her head. "I can't let you pay for my hairdo. I've got this."

"Oh no. I know how cheap you are —"

Danetta held up a hand. "Frugal . . . not cheap."

"Okay, Ms. Frugal. I'm paying because you are getting a cut and color. You're also getting your nails done, a pedicure and that bush you call eyebrows waxed. I'm going to drop Jaylen off at my mom's, and then I'll be back, so don't try to chicken out of anything," Ryla said, as she pulled the keys out of her purse and headed toward the door.

"Ryla already picked the style and color that she thought would look best on you. So, the question is, do you trust your girl or not?" Marlene asked.

Danetta looked at her reflection in the salon's mirror. She was tired of her ponytail also, but just didn't know what hairstyle she wanted. "Since I have no idea what hairstyle will look best on me, I guess I'll have to trust her."

"Yea!" Marlene clapped her hands like a giddy schoolgirl. "Let's get this party started." She pulled the rubber band from around Danetta's ponytail and threw it in the trash. She then put a cape around Danetta and a plastic bag with holes in it on her head.

As Marlene began pulling strands of Danetta's hair through the holes in the plastic bag, Danetta scrunched up her face. "That doesn't feel so good. Why do you have to pull my hair through those tiny holes?"

"Girl, haven't you ever had highlights before?"

"What's that?"

"Danetta, Danetta, Danetta, what am I going to do with you?" Marlene asked while shaking her head. Then she began to explain, "I'm going to put this golden-bronze color in your hair. Since your hair is a dark brown, this color is going to lighten your hair up quite a bit, so we're not going to do a full head of color. I'm pulling the strands of hair through the holes, because I'm only going to color the hair on the outside of the bag. All the rest of your hair will mostly remain the same color. But the colored strands will highlight your hair in a dramatic way."

It took all the strength Danetta had to stay glued to her seat. She wasn't sure if she could handle anything dramatic. And what would her clients say when she showed up at work with golden-bronze highlights?

"You look nervous, hon. What's up? Speak now, before it's too late," Marlene warned.

"This just seems like such a drastic change all at once," Danetta admitted.

"From what Ryla told me, it sounded as if you were looking for a change. Is that right?"

No, that's not right, Danetta wanted to scream. She wanted a man, not a new hairdo. But maybe Ryla didn't think she'd be able to get a man unless she made a drastic change to her appearance. Plus, she did ask for Ryla's help. She leaned back in her seat. "Yeah, I guess that's right."

For the next few hours, Danetta moved from one salon chair to the next, getting color, a cut, a French manicure, a pedicure and her eyebrows waxed. When Ryla walked back into the salon, she did a double take as she stared at the vision in front of her.

"Danetta, girl, you are smokin' hot."

Danetta touched her hair as she glanced in the mirror, then she moved her head from side to side. The cut was an improvement from the ponytail she'd been sporting. It brought out the intensity in her eyes. Danetta didn't just look like another pretty face, the style was boardroom savvy and she liked that. But she wondered if the cut was too much about business and not enough about her as a woman. "You don't think she cut off too much of my hair?"

"The layered look fits you. And your hair is not short at all. It's shoulder length."

"Yeah, but my hair used to flow down my back. I thought men liked women with long hair?"

Ryla received the bill and then paid the receptionist. She turned back to Danetta and said, "Trust me, you still have enough hair to make any man happy."

"What about the highlights? Do you think it's too much? Should I get it toned down a bit?" Danetta peered in the mirror. She didn't know if she could get use to the shimmery color that caught the sunlight every time she moved her head.

"Don't change a thing," Ryla argued. "You'll see just how much this new 'do suits you, once we get everything else in place.

Now come on, we've got some shopping to do."

"Shopping? Oh no, Ryla. You know I hate shopping," Danetta complained. "I wanted you to come over to my house and help me mix and match some outfits in my closet."

"Girl, we are going to throw some of those tired, old, granny clothes in the trash. Now, come on. You can ride with me, and then I'll bring you back to get your car when we're done."

Danetta hesitated. "I'm not so sure I need to go this far."

"Look, you've got the dinner cruise coming up. And take it from me, girlfriend, upgrading your wardrobe will be like bringing the honey to the bee," Ryla said while snapping her fingers. "And anyway, the dinner cruise is an old-school event, and I know you don't own anything from the '70s or '80s."

"I'm going to wear this flower-child dress I wore to a costume party a few years ago."

"Look, Danetta," Ryla said firmly. "Every one of your clients purchased an extra ticket to give to a business associate of their choice. Simply put, your future husband could be attending this event. And since I'm the party planner this year, I refuse to let you attend this event in a flower child's dress."

Ryla worked full-time at an energy company as director of the marketing department. However, a year ago she started a party planning business on the side. So, Danetta decided to help her friend out by providing her with some business. For the past four years, she and Marshall had been hosting a Valentine's Day event for their clients. The event also served as an annual fundraiser, from which the proceeds went to the local charity of Danetta's choice. This year, Destiny Home for Girls would be receiving the funds collected.

Every year, Marshall arrived with a beautiful goddess on his arm. Since Danetta hadn't been asked on a Valentine's date in years, she normally brought Surry or Ryla so that they could get their networking on. The fact that this event would be held the weekend following Valentine's Day, eased a bit of the I-need-a-special-occasion-date pressure. However, watching Marshall play with his latest black Barbie doll always made Danetta feel frumpy and dumpy. But Danetta was throwing frumpy off a cliff this year. She couldn't wait to see Marshall's reaction to her new look. "All right, let's go," she said as she got in Ryla's car.

CHAPTER 4

What was wrong with women these days?
Marshall wondered as he stretched out on
the king-size bed in his hotel room, completely alone. He had high hopes of meeting
up with a fine sistah and spending about
twelve hours of quality time with her. But
he'd been knocked off his game and didn't
have the energy to pursue another woman.

First Veronica busts up the ceramic lamp
Danetta bought him for Christmas, then
the crazy woman keyed his car just because
he was okay with her breaking up with him.
What was he supposed to do, cry over
her . . . call and beg her for another chance?

Then this woman whose name he couldn't
even remember hauls off and slaps him just
because he hadn't bothered to call her after
they'd spent one night together. *Who does
that? I mean, come on. If a woman slips up
and sleeps with a man the first day they meet,
does that woman really believe that any man*

*in his right mind is about to rush home and
call her?* Marshall considered himself to be
a polite man whose mama raised him right.
So, he was sure that he thanked ol' what's-
her-name before she left his hotel room.
"Abalit, balit, that's all folks."

He was no different from any other full-
grown, unattached man. He liked the ladies
but he liked to keep things free and loose
— he wasn't a puppet, so he made sure that
no strings were attached to him. As long as
everyone was having a good time all was
fine. What he couldn't deal with was the
keying cars and slapping-brothers-in-public
type of women.

He put his hands behind his head as he
mused that maybe he'd slipped up on his
application process with those two, or
maybe the game was just growing old. After
all, he was thirty-two years old and his
mother had started throwing hints about
grandchildren. Maybe it was time for him
to settle down. He just needed to find one
woman and make it happen. In truth,
Marshall had dated hundreds of women,
but not one of them came to mind when he
thought of the woman he'd like to have a
few babies with.

Danetta and Ryla spent the rest of the day

looking for clothes that didn't make her look, as Ryla said, like "a tired old granny."

"If you want a man to be interested, you need to let him see what you're working with," Ryla said as she put back a dress that Danetta thought was perfect.

"What's wrong with that dress?" She pointed at the shapeless cloth hanging on the hanger.

"It's too long and it billows out at the waistline," Ryla criticized. "Need I say more?"

As if a lightbulb finally came on, Danetta smiled, saying, "No one would be able to see my curves in that dress."

"Exactly. Now this little number is designed get a man's attention in a hurry." Ryla lifted a black nightclub dress off the rack. The fabric was stretchy and designed to be formfitting so it would show off every curve. The quarter-length sleeves and one side of the hem had been slashed so many times, the dress could have been made by Freddy Krueger.

Danetta's eyes widened as she said, "Ryla Evans, if you don't put that dress back, I'm ending this shopping trip right now."

Laughing, Ryla put the dress back on the rack. "Hey, I was just trying to see how desperate for a man you really are."

"Would you wear something like that?"

"Not in this life," Ryla admitted.

"Then why on earth would you think I would go anywhere in a dress like that? It's way too revealing."

"You're the one looking for a man," Ryla joked. "The last thing on my mind is some knuckleheaded man, so I don't have to worry about dressing to impress."

"Ryla, everything you wear is stylish. And whether you know it or not, you attract men to you all day long. Why do you think I asked for your help?"

Ryla put her finger to her chin as she took a moment to think. "Okay, then I'm going to take you to Galleria Mall. My mom and I shop there every time she comes to Houston. You'll love it."

They drove over to Galleria Mall and Danetta got excited when she found a two hundred and fifty dollar Donna Karan dress that had been marked down to fifty dollars. The dress enhanced her curves, but did not make her look like a stripper. She rarely found deals at the Galleria, so she snatched that dress up real quick. Then they went to Stein Mart, and Danetta found several other outfits. When she was tired of shopping for clothes, Ryla told her that they needed to make one more stop.

As they stood in front of the cosmetic counter, Danetta thought about changing her mind. She thought that if she needed to change that much just to get a man, then maybe she was okay being alone for the rest of her life. Just then a woman pushing a baby stroller walked past her. Danetta looked inside the stroller and watched the baby cooing as she lifted her chubby little legs in the air. That was all it took. She felt like she didn't have very many baby-making years left, so she wasn't going to waste her time complaining about a little makeup if that's what it took to attract her husband.

Danetta's face held no blemishes whatsoever, which was one of the reasons that she'd never bothered with foundation. So she asked the makeup artist, "Do I really need foundation if I don't have any freckles or blemishes to cover up?"

The woman smiled. "Foundation serves as a base for all the other makeup that we will put on your face, it helps to smooth everything out. And you are correct that you don't need a heavy foundation. But we have a light coverage that will work for your face. Would you like to try it?"

"Yes, she would," Ryla responded before Danetta could answer. "The foundation she needs should have a natural finish with golden/olive undertones." Ryla spoke as if she'd worked as a makeup artist herself.

The correct shade of foundation was applied to Danetta's honey-toned skin. Then came the eye shadow, blush and a pinky-brown lip gloss. All the things that Danetta felt were so unnecessary for daily living. However, when the makeup was applied, and Danetta held the mirror and looked at her reflection, she was stunned at the vision she saw. "I-I look beautiful!"

"If Marshall Windham could see you now, he'd turn in his playa card and become a do-right man," Ryla said, with a knowing glint in her eye.

"Don't kid yourself. Marshall has seen me dressed for awards banquets and business dinners. The man wants nothing from me but friendship."

"He hasn't seen you like this, Danetta. No one has." Ryla took her digital camera out of her purse and snapped a few shots. "Don't get the big head, but girl, you clean up real good."

Danetta felt herself blush. "Thanks, Ryla. I never had on this much makeup before, and I never imagined that a new hairdo and some makeup could make this much of a difference."

"Come on," Ryla said, "We've got one last

thing to do before I can get back home to my child."

Danetta purchased all the cosmetics that were used for her makeover and then turned to walk out of the store. Two men were in front of the store having conversations with the women who were with them as Danetta and Ryla walked out. As if by sheer force of nature, both men stopped talking and turned their heads, staring in Danetta's and Ryla's direction.

"See what I mean, Ryla . . . those men will even risk the wrath of the women they are with just to stare at you."

Ryla looked over at the men and laughed. "I don't know how to break this to you, Danetta, but those men aren't staring at me; they're looking directly at you."

Unable to fathom that any man would be staring at her while Ryla was with her, Danetta turned to see for herself. One of the men winked at her and the woman he was with punched him in the stomach and then turned and started screaming at Danetta.

Ryla grabbed Danetta's arm, and they ran to her car. Once inside they looked at each other and began laughing hysterically. As they drove off, the woman was still fussing. "Can you believe she is mad at me? I didn't tell her man to wink at me," Danetta said.

"You didn't have to. I told you before, these mongrels do just what they want to do."

"Ryla, don't you think it's about time you stopped calling every man you meet a mongrel? There are some good men in this world."

"Well, I don't know any of them," Ryla said and then held up a hand to halt the conversation. "But don't let my bitterness dissuade you. If a man is what you want, then I will help you find one . . . mongrel or not."

Shaking her head, Danetta leaned back in her seat. It amazed her that Ryla was so beautiful and yet so bitter at times. Danetta knew that Jaylen's father had something to do with her friend's attitude toward men, but Ryla never talked about him and she didn't want to pry.

Ryla dropped Danetta off at the salon so she could pick up her car. "I'll meet you at your house, so we can work on the final phase of our little Get Love Now plan."

Danetta drove home anxious to discover what Ryla had planned next. If the changes her friend had suggested so far were able to garner her stares and a wink, she wondered what the final phase would bring. Danetta had high hopes that it would bring the husband and the baby carriage.

"Okay, so what's next?" Danetta asked, once she had brought all of her new clothes and cosmetics into the house.

"Turn on your computer," Ryla instructed.

"Has it been so long for the both of us that we need to research how to find a man?" Danetta joked as they sat in front of her computer.

"Oh no, my sistah, I know how to find a man. And I am going to show you just how to do it quickly." Ryla turned to Danetta and asked, "You did say that you didn't have much time to waste, right?"

"Right."

"Okay, then the first thing I need is a USB cable so I can download the pictures I took of you at the mall."

Danetta opened her desk drawer and produced the cable.

Ryla then downloaded the pictures of Danetta from her camera onto her computer. "Sign in to Facebook."

"What for?" Danetta asked.

"You'll see once you get there."

Danetta did as she was told and then relinquished her seat to Ryla. Ryla then uploaded the picture of Danetta that showed her all dolled up, to replace the one she currently had on her profile. Her previous profile picture showed Danetta with no makeup and her usual ponytail. She was holding a briefcase, looking like she was posing for Business Woman of the Year or something. Ryla updated Danetta's info page to say that she was single and interested in men. She also changed her status to say, "Today I'm single, tomorrow . . . who knows?"

"Why'd you do that? Now I'm going to have a bunch of men bothering me."

"I thought you wanted to be bothered?" Ryla lifted an eyebrow, daring Danetta to make more of a fuss.

"Well, yeah, but there's no need to advertise that fact, is there?"

"If you want to find a man quickly, we need to advertise. As a matter of fact, we are getting ready to sign you up on Black PeopleMeet.com."

Danetta began shaking her head. "I don't think I can do that, Ryla." She stood up. "I don't know, maybe this is too much . . . too fast."

Before Ryla could respond, an instant message popped up on Danetta's computer from someone named Frank. He said hello and informed Danetta that he liked her new picture and would like to get to know her better.

Danetta's mouth hung open as she looked at the message. "What is wrong with this man? He doesn't even know me."

"Welcome to the digital age. This is the way people meet in the twenty-first century."

"No, it's not. I've met men at the grocery store or in a parking lot," Danetta replied.

"And how's that working out for you?" Ryla could barely keep the sarcasm out of her voice. "How many dates have you been on with the men you've met in parking lots or at the grocery store?"

Danetta thought about that for a moment. When she came up with a big fat zero, she leaned in to her computer and checked out Frank's picture. "He's kind of cute, isn't he?"

"Sure is. Can I respond to him?"

Being more decisive, Danetta said, "Yes, ask him where he works."

Ryla shook her head and rolled her eyes at that suggestion. "That's something you can ask later. Right now we want to know if he lives anywhere near Houston." So, Ryla asked if he lived in Texas.

Frank turned out to be an Ohio resident, and Danetta felt that he was just too far away. So, they logged out of Facebook and went to BlackPeopleMeet.com. Ryla uploaded Danetta's picture and filled out her profile. She then turned to Danetta and said, "Okay, you should begin getting some hits on Facebook and BlackPeopleMeet .com tonight or tomorrow. All you have to do is decide which of the respondents you want to go out with."

Danetta bent over and gave Ryla a hug. "Thank you so much, Ryla. I don't think I could have done any of this without you."

"Don't thank me yet. You could end up married to some brother who can't even see the letters *j-o-b* without having a panic attack."

Danetta laughed. "Go on somewhere with that kind of talk. My Aunt Sarah spends too much time praying for me for something like that to happen."

CHAPTER 5

"My girl has another friend who wants to hook up with you," Kevin Underwood said as he and Marshall jogged on the treadmill.

"The last friend of your girl's that you hooked me up with keyed my car . . . No thank you."

Kevin hit the stop button on his treadmill, jerked to a stop and turned to face Marshall with openmouthed disbelief. "Veronica keyed your car?"

Marshall nodded but kept his jog going.

"When?" Kevin asked as he reset the treadmill so he could walk fast and talk.

"This past weekend. She got mad because I changed my mind about taking her out of town with me."

"Did you call the police?"

"Naw, I thought about it but —" Marshall paused as he puffed out his chest and slowed his jog. "I've got a reputation to uphold . . . can't be running to the police like I'm scared of some girl."

"Yeah, I feel you," Kevin said as he laughed at the thought.

They finished up on the treadmill and then hit the showers. Marshall and Kevin had been working out three days a week together since college. They normally lifted weights, but this morning, neither man had the energy, so they elected to do a cardio workout. Not that skipping the weights would hurt either of them; both men had broad shoulders, washboard abs and muscular arms and legs that caused a *lawd-have-mercy* from a few women as they walked by.

Once they were dressed in their business suits, looking like they were ready to take on the world, Marshall headed toward his Lincoln SUV, while Kevin headed toward the black on black Lexus parked next to it.

"So are we going to the club tomorrow? It's ladies' night," Kevin offered.

Marshall shook his head. "Naw, man, I'm getting tired of clubbing."

"Since when has a club full of hoochies ever tired you out?"

"I'm getting too old for hoochies and my mama always used to tell me that if I want something different, I have to do something different."

"Boy you sound like Forrest Gump . . . M-my mama said . . . my mama said," Kevin laughed.

"Chuckle it up, homeboy, but I'm serious. These last few knuckleheads that I've dated have caused me to realize that I need a stable-minded woman, rather than these flakes I've been dealing with."

For the second time that morning, Marshall said something that caused Kevin to stop in his tracks. "Say it ain't so. Don't tell me that Marshall Windham is getting ready to turn in his playa card?"

"Nobody said anything about turning in my membership. I'm gon' keep my man cave . . . just looking to hang out with a woman who has common sense." Marshall would never tell Kevin about the woman he ran into at the business retreat, but her words had really gotten to him. Marshall looked into that beautiful woman's eyes and saw how much he had hurt her. Truth be told, it bothered him to know that his actions had caused such pain to another human being.

Kevin snapped his fingers. "You know who would be perfect for you?"

Shaking his head, Marshall said, "I don't need a hook-up. I can handle mine."

"Shut up, fool, I'm not trying to hook you

up. I'm talking about Danetta."

Marshall stopped, stared at his friend. "Danetta who?"

"Danetta Harris, your business partner . . . who do you think I'm talking about?"

Marshall shook his head and started walking toward his SUV again.

"What's wrong with Danetta? You and her get along, you like the same things. Heck, she even roots for the same sorry sports teams that you do."

"That's the exact problem. Other than you, Danetta is the best friend that I have. I can't mess that up by getting into a relationship with her."

Kevin thought a moment. "You're probably right. Most of your women do become disgruntled by the time they leave."

"What you talkin' 'bout, man? I leave my women happy and satisfied," Marshall said with a little extra swag in his walk.

As they reached their cars in the parking lot, both Marshall and Kevin stood there for a moment looking as if their favorite dog had just been run over while they stood and watched it happen. Then as if Marshall's head exploded, he began jumping up and down as he ran around his SUV. "She flattened three of my tires! Didn't I tell you . . . didn't I tell you, man? That woman is ten kinds of crazy."

"Dawg, naw!" Kevin put his hands over his mouth and kept staring at the destruction before him.

Marshall flailed his arms back and forth. "What am I supposed to do now?"

"This ain't happy and satisfied, man." Kevin shook his head. "It's time for you to say something."

Lowering his head as if lowering his pride, Marshall asked, "Can you give me a ride to the police station?"

Heads swiveled and twirled around as Danetta strutted into work on Monday morning.

"You look really nice today, Danetta. I love the haircut," Monica, her assistant, said as she passed her in the hallway.

"Thank you." Danetta pulled her oversized Coach bag over her shoulder and continued toward her office like a woman on a mission.

By the time Monday morning rolled around, she had grown comfortable with her look and knew she looked good. The hair and makeup were positive changes and Danetta owed Ryla big time for helping her with it. But she still wasn't so sure about the new clothes. Danetta had a strict "no cleavage" policy when it came to the work-place. But she had listened to Ryla and ignored her best judgment; now she was being ogled and stared at like she was a work-on-your-back kind of girl. She rushed to her office and dialed Ryla's number. As the phone rang, she noticed the single red rose in the crystal vase that had been placed on her desk. She shook her head as she frowned at the rose that Marshall sent to her. He gave her a single red rose every February 13th. Years ago, she had asked him to stop sending her that single red rose the day before Valentine's Day because it only served to remind her that she didn't have anyone special in her life. No one had ever sent her the full dozen on the most romantic day of the year. Marshall had assured her that someone would come along and out-shine his single red rose, but until they did, he would continue letting her know that she was cherished.

But even that bugged Danetta, because being cherished was a world away from being loved. The phone rang three times and then as her friend picked up she said, "Why did I let you talk me into this? I feel like I'm Lil' Kim or Mariah Carey. It's like I just walked into my office with ten pounds of extra boobs that I didn't have last week or something."

"Girl, hush, I'm sure you look quite respectable. Your boobs are not exposed in any of the outfits we picked out, your curves are just a little more defined, that's all. You just feel uncomfortable because you're used to wearing those turtlenecks and high-collar shirts."

"I don't know, Ryla," she said as she looked down at the crimson colored V-neck, Ann Taylor blouse with the twist knot detail displayed just below her boobs, which was the reason she felt as if that particular body part was being highlighted. "Maybe I should go home and change before my date."

"You'll do no such thing. Your date will be thanking his lucky stars that a woman like you chose to spend her lunch break with him . . . Has Marshall seen you yet?"

She glanced at her watch and then at the rose. "No. We're supposed to meet in about an hour to go over any leads he came up with at the business retreat this weekend. We also need to go over last-minute details for Friday night's dinner cruise."

"Okay, well I'll let you go so you can get ready for your meeting."

Danetta sighed. "Okay, Ryla, I'll talk to you later."

"And Danetta, do me a favor."

"What's that?"

"Relax and just be beautiful today, all right?"

Danetta took a deep breath and exhaled. She had always just been the smart girl with glasses. Men didn't look at her with lust-filled eyes. They came to her when they needed facts and figures. "Okay, Ryla, I'll relax."

She hung up the phone, picked up a pen and began tapping it on her desk as she searched for something that would help her relax. Neither coffee, tea nor chocolate relaxed Danetta. She didn't kick up her feet and cozy up with a good book when she needed to unwind. It had always been work and more work that stopped her mind from racing into a hundred different directions. Her work allowed her to focus by concentrating on abstract things. She grabbed a couple of files and got down to business.

But Danetta's thoughts kept drifting back to Mark Joseph, the guy she was having lunch with today. She met him on Facebook over the weekend, and readily accepted his offer of lunch. She hoped that she hadn't seemed too eager, but Danetta had been so singularly focused on her career that she hadn't been on a date in years. And she'd spent all those years, dreaming about Marshall. Now she needed a new dream.

Danetta picked up the phone and called Destiny Home for Girls to ensure that the director of the home for troubled teens would still be able to attend their annual fundraiser/Valentine's Day event. When she hung up with the director, she got to work on the final details for the weekend event.

She had become so engrossed in her work that it wasn't until a little after eleven o'clock that she noticed Marshall hadn't shown up for their morning meeting. She picked up the phone to dial his office, but then thought better of it. If Marshall wanted to blow off their meeting, then so be it. She had things to do and no time to worry about him today. She stood up and went to the file cabinet to pull out the information on the dinner cruise. She needed to make sure that their clients would have a fabulous time and then, hopefully, want to continue doing business with them. She bent over to pull the material out of the third drawer.

Marshall poked his head in her office and asked, "Hey, where's . . ." When he recognized Danetta, he nearly stuttered. "What'd you do with my girl, Danetta Harris?"

Danetta grabbed the documents she'd been looking for and stood up. She turned toward Marshall and said, "I have a lot of work to do this morning, so I don't have time for foolishness right now."

Marshall's head did a twirl and a swivel as Danetta sauntered back to her desk. "What do you have on?" he asked as he walked into the office and sat down in the chair in front of her desk.

"Clothes."

"I can see that. But *you* don't wear things like *that.*" He pointed at her. "Your outfits are normally a bit more loose fitting."

Slamming the files on her desk she rolled her eyes heavenward. "It's none of your business what I have on, Marshall. Why don't you go ask one of your girlfriends about their attire and leave mine alone?"

Raising a hand to surrender, Marshall said, "Whoa. I didn't mean to get you all riled up. I'm just simply trying to say —" he leaned back and studied her for a moment "— dang girl, you look good . . . real good. But this it not you. Ryla, put you up to this, didn't she?"

Danetta gasped. Marshall thought he knew her so well. At times, he'd even said things to her that made her wonder if he had a gift for reading minds. Whether he was on to something or not, there was no way she would admit that her new look wasn't her own idea. She changed subjects.

"Is there some reason why you're in my office?"

"We had a meeting scheduled, remember?"

Danetta looked at her watch, then turned toward Marshall so he could view the time for himself. "You're two hours late. Oh, and didn't I ask you to stop sending these single roses to me?"

"You're welcome," he said as if she had thanked him. "And I had a little car trouble." *And psycho-stalker woman trouble.*

"Don't you have a cell phone?"

"My mind was on a thousand different things, D. I'm sorry. I just forgot to call you."

Hardly believing his excuse, she continued, "Well, we'll have to reschedule our meeting. I'm trying to finish up some last-minute details for the dinner cruise."

"No problem." Marshall stood up, leaned over her desk and inhaled the rose.

Still irritated, Danetta asked, "Why on earth do you continue to send me a rose the day before Valentine's Day? Don't you know that it just makes me feel inadequate" She almost told him that she felt alone because she didn't have anyone special sending her flowers, but she would never admit that.

"It makes you feel what?"

Turning away from him, she said, "Nothing . . . Forget I said anything."

"I hope it makes you feel cherished, because I cherish our friendship and just want to show you how much, every now and again."

"You don't have to do this. I'm perfectly fine without it."

He raised his hands as if surrendering. "Okay, I can see that my missing our meeting has put you in a mood. So let me take you to lunch and I'll tell you all about the big fish I just reeled into our company."

"No can do."

Marshall stopped walking and did an about-face, as he turned back toward Danetta. "Since when do you turn down a free lunch?"

Head still buried in her files, she said, "Since I have a lunch date."

"A lunch date?" He said the words as if they scorched his tongue on the way out of his mouth. "With who?"

Danetta put her pen down as she looked up at Marshall and said, "With none of your business, that's who."

Her cell phone rang. Danetta picked it up and hit the talk button. "This is Danetta Harris . . . oh, okay, I'll be right down." She hit the end button and then stood up. As she walked past him she said, "If you're not busy this afternoon, we can meet when I get back."

"All right, I'll walk you out," Marshall said as he followed Danetta out of her office.

"You don't need to do that."

"Nonsense. As your business partner and friend, the least I can do is escort you to your date."

"Whatever," Danetta said as she hit the down button for the elevator.

"I'm serious, D. I don't want you going out with any old blockhead. You need a man who knows how special you are."

Really? Her voice dripped with sarcasm, because Danetta knew for a fact that Marshall Windham had no clue how special she was. Danetta was sick of waiting on Marshall or worrying about what he thought of her. She was going to live her life and find someone who wanted to live it with her.

The elevator arrived, they got in and Danetta moved to the back and leaned against the wall. She could feel Marshall's eyes on her, but she didn't turn in his direction.

"So," he began. "I guess you wore this dress for your date, huh?"

"Why are you so concerned with my

clothes all of a sudden?"

He studied her before the elevator door opened and as they walked out together.

Marshall said, "You surprised me, D. In college, all you ever wore was sweatshirts and oversized T-shirts with sweats or jeans. In the office, you normally have on these boring pantsuits with long, straight jackets. I just didn't know."

"Know what?" she asked confused by the way he ended his statement.

His eyes swept over her backside as he said, "Baby got back."

"Shut up, Marshall." She pushed him. But as she headed toward the door she wondered if she had truly just seen the look of desire in Marshall's eyes. No way, she was imagining things. Marshall was just shocked by her new look. That's it and that's all.

He opened the door for her. She walked out and stood at the curb waiting for her date to pull up. Her date was driving a burgundy Chevy Impala. As he pulled up and got out of the car, Marshall whispered in her ear, "Respectable car for a woman, but most of the men I know wouldn't drive it."

"Not everyone was born wealthy. Some people have to take what they can get and be happy," Danetta shot back and then

71

turned to the man she would be having lunch with. He wasn't dressed in a business suit like Marshall, but his polo shirt and slacks hung nicely on him. She smiled. "Hi, Mark."

Mark stopped in front of her, gawked at her like a schoolboy. "Wow, you look even better than your Facebook picture."

Marshall grabbed her arm. "You met this guy on Facebook? Do you know how dangerous that is?"

Pulling away from Marshall, she said to Mark, "It's nice to meet you in person."

"Likewise," Mark said and then he stuck his hand out to Marshall. "I'm Mark Joseph."

"Marshall Windham."

"I'll just get my car out of the parking lot and follow you," Danetta said.

"Oh, yeah, sure." Mark got back into his car and waited for Danetta to pull up behind him.

As Danetta pulled up behind Mark, she noticed that Marshall was still standing in front of the building. She waved at him as she drove off. In her rearview mirror she watched Marshall wave back at her. The look on his face puzzled her and caused her to wonder why he continued to stand there waving, looking like a little lost puppy, instead of the mongrel Ryla says he was.

CHAPTER 6

Danetta stepped onto the dinner boat at four o'clock, an hour before the guests were to arrive. The event normally lasted from five until eight, with most guests leaving around seven-thirty. Some guests hung around until around eight-thirty, not leaving until the cleanup crew showed up. Danetta felt as if she had the most in common with those guests . . . the ones who had nowhere else to be . . . no one to spend the weekend with.

Turning away from her thoughts, she began scanning the room to ensure that all of her instructions had been followed. Since this was an old-school party, a big disco ball was dangling from the center of the dance floor. The food was out on display . . . shrimp, crab legs, lobster salad, roast beef, vegetables of all colors and variations, and cakes and pies lined the tables. In the middle of the decadent array of food sat an ice sculpture with the Windham Enterprises logo carved into it. Everything was beautiful.

The best part of this annual dinner party had nothing to do with the decorations or the food. It occurred when Danetta presented a plaque and a check to a local nonprofit organization. Too many organizations that provided valuable services within the community were closing their doors due to lack of funds. So, even though the ten thousand dollars she collected from ticket sales wouldn't keep the doors open for an entire year, Danetta knew full well that the money would be appreciated.

She turned to her left to view the display table she had asked her assistant to set up. This event not only catered to current clients, but also focused on bringing in new business, which was a tough feat to accomplish when they didn't actually do business at their annual dinner party. Still, Danetta made sure that their ad campaigns from the previous year were on display in big, bold Texas style.

Last year, Windham Enterprises landed several local and national television commercials. They'd done countless billboard ads and internet advertising for their clients. She couldn't fit all of their campaigns on the table, but she made sure to highlight the important ones. Brochures also lined the table with more information concerning their firm and all of the other clients they handled in the previous year.

"Diva."

Danetta heard Ryla's voice and turned to greet her friend. She was struck by how beautiful Ryla looked in her '70s getup. The woman had on a psychedelic go-go-girl jumpsuit that cut off just below her J-Lo booty, with a pair of white, knee-high go-go boots. "Girl, you are rocking those boots."

Ryla smiled as she twirled around. "I thought I'd do a little something-something. But look at you. Diva, you are not only rocking your go-go boots . . . you are doing the darn thang with that dress."

This was the first time Danetta had ever received a compliment for wearing a 100% polyester dress. But she had to admit that the rainbow swirl dress with matching head wrap and bell sleeves showed off her legs and her curves, since the dress was form-fitting and so tight that she had to suck in her stomach in order to get into it. "Thanks for helping me pick this dress out, Ryla. The dress I had planned on wearing wouldn't have been as much fun as this one."

Ryla rolled her eyes. "Thank God I took

you shopping. I would have hated to see you in that long, ugly dress you wanted to wear."

Danetta playfully shoved her friend. "Hey, no fair talking about my clothes. But I do appreciate your help. I can't even tell you how many men tried to holler at me as I walked down the plank to get on this boat."

"Their tongues were hanging out of their mouths when I came in also. Let's just hope that those guys don't try to crash the party." As if dismissing the thought of men and their ignorant ways, Ryla turned Danetta toward the seating area on the boat. "So, what do you think?"

Danetta had already checked out the disco ball, but now as she looked around, Danetta noticed the multicolored roses that had been set in the center of each round table. Ryla had even placed psychedelic napkins on the tables and multicolored beanbags around the room. "I guess we'll just have to call you, Ms. Party Planner Extraordinaire."

"You haven't seen anything yet. When the lights go down in this place and the DJ starts playing all that old-school music, and people go back down memory lane . . . I'm telling you, Danetta, your clients are going to be talking about this party for years to come."

"The music will definitely set the mood for them. Marshall barely remembers anything about the '70s, because he was in diapers until 1979, but he still loves the music from the time period. He even keeps his car radio on an oldies station."

"Well it's going to be '70s and '80s music popping off in here, so he'll love it."

"I'm sure his date will too," Danetta said with a frown on her face.

Ryla put her arm around Danetta and started to say something, but the door opened and Surry strutted in.

"What's up, my sistahs?" Surry called out as she stepped into the room looking like a '70s model on the catwalk with her gray-and-silver disco pantsuit with bell-bottom sleeves and pants. Her Angela Davis afro swayed as if a breeze blew by with each step she took in her platform shoes.

Danetta put her hands on her hips as she pretended to reprimand Surry. "Girl, how dare you come in here looking better than me?"

"And me too," Ryla said with hands on her hips.

"Both of you need to quit it because we are three beautiful women. I just hope the men coming to this party appreciate that fact." Surry then turned to Danetta and said, "And there had better be more dark-skinned men in attendance this year, or I just might lose my mind and ask Marshall for a dance."

"We don't determine our guest list based on your dating profile, Surry," Danetta teased. "So, you'll just have to get over your militant attitude about light-skinned men and maybe have a conversation with one or two."

Surry made a gagging sound. "I told you before, I don't want nothing white or light, but my Wonder bread."

"I keep trying to figure out what could've happened to turn you so completely against light-skinned brothers. Maybe it was some childhood trauma," Ryla said, grinning at her dig.

"Don't psychoanalyze me tonight, Ryla," Surry said, sounding a bit deflated. "I just broke up with Joe, so I'd rather you spent your time helping me find a chocolate brother to spend the evening with."

"What happened with you and Joe?" Danetta asked.

"He was crowding me."

Danetta shook her head. "Girl, if I didn't know better, I'd swear you were a man in drag. What I wouldn't give for some man to crowd me." The three women laughed.

The doors opened again and the first group of guests began arriving. Danetta and Ryla started handing out their business cards, while Surry searched for another dark and handsome man to use and abuse.

"You're kidding, right?" Marshall asked as he looked at the getup Kevin had on. "I know that your boss does not want you to pass out business cards with the name of his company on it while you are wearing a lime green-and-purple mack daddy suit."

"My boss is just fine with the way I'm dressed. You're just mad because you're wearing those tired old retro bell-bottoms and a shirt with a long collar like the guys on *Sanford and Son* used to wear."

Marshall looked down at his outfit. "Hey, I like my shirt." It was aqua, black and white with swirls all over it. "Okay, man, my outfit might not be as flamboyant as yours, but this is a business function, with clients that I represent. At least I'm coming correct."

Kevin leaned back, opened his lime green coat jacket and twirled around. "That's why I'm representing all the playas. I figure that if somebody has to do it . . . might as well be me."

Laughing, Marshall said, "All right, all right, be a playa if you want to, but please take off that dollar sign medallion. It's bigger than any chain Mr. T ever dreamed of wearing."

Kevin took the silver medallion off his neck and handed it to Marshall. "Here, you take it. You'll need some bling with that tired outfit you're wearing."

Marshall put the medallion on and then stepped back and posed. "How do I look?"

"Like an old-school hustler." Kevin straightened out Marshall's collar as he added, "You just might pull a few women at this event. That is, if I don't pull them first."

"Boy, shut up. If you even try to get a number that's not business related, I'm going to turn snitch and tell your girl Marla everything I know."

"Don't forget that I have Veronica's number. I'll call her up and remind her that she forgot to slash that fourth tire."

Marshall got in his car. Kevin sat on the passenger side of the car and as Marshall started the engine he said, "I'm not even thinking about Veronica. I have enough on my mind just trying to figure Danetta out."

"What's up with Danetta?"

"She's mad at me," he confessed.

"Again, what did you do this time?"

Rolling his eyes while driving towards the event. "I committed the cardinal sin of buying her a rose the day before Valentine's Day."

Kevin put his hand to his ear. "Run that by me again."

"I'm serious, man. I buy Danetta a single red rose every February 13. She normally just says thank you and then we go on about our day. But she freaked out about it this time. Then she went out to lunch with some lame dude. I thought she would be in a better mood when she came back to work but she still wasn't speaking to me. She even refused to meet with me to discuss business."

"If the guy was lame, she might have been mad about wasting her lunch break on him."

"Naw, she's definitely mad at me. I just don't know why."

"Well, maybe she wants the rose on Valentine's Day rather than the day before."

Marshall thought about that for a moment, then said, "I just didn't want things to be awkward between us." When Kevin gave him a look that indicated he had no clue what Marshall was talking about he continued, "You know . . . flowers on Valentine's Day are for lovers. So, I always get Danetta a flower the day before."

"Yeah, but if it's making her mad, why do you even bother giving her the rose at all?"

He shrugged yet kept his eyes on the road. "It's just that sometimes I get the impression that Danetta is lonely. I don't think she's had a date on Valentine's Day in years, and I just want her to know that she is special . . . even if some of these other knuckleheads haven't figured it out yet."

"Marshall, my brother, I don't know what's been going on with you lately, but you're slipping." Kevin shook his head. "Even I know that you don't give a red rose to a woman that you're not knocking boots with."

Marshall ignored Kevin as he continued driving to their destination. When they finally arrived at the dinner boat, Marshall looked at Kevin's outfit again, shook his head and then got out of the car.

Kevin got out of the car and asked, "What was that look for?"

"You're dressed like Antonio Fargas from the *I'm Gonna Git You Sucka* movie. All that's missing is the fish in your shoes."

Kevin started strutting toward the boat. "Don't hate. Celebrate."

"Okay mack daddy, we're going to see just how many women celebrate this getup you got on," Marshall said as he stepped onto the boat. He then opened the door and walked into the lower level of the boat where the party had already gotten started. The lights were dim, the disco ball was lit and twirled around, casting shadows and a multitude of colors on everyone on the dance floor.

"Oh, it's jumping in here," Kevin said as he popped his fingers to "Dance to the Music" by Sly & the Family Stone.

Marshall turned around and checked out all the smiling faces that stood in the food line, stuffing their plates with shrimp, crab legs, pasta and any and everything else to be had. He looked at the display table which held small, medium and large-size posters with designs that Windham Enterprises had done for clients the previous year. Marshall had been against the whole idea of a display table, but year after year, new clients contacted their firm because of the information they obtained from that table. At this very moment, he counted ten people hovering around the display table, and not just any ten people . . . ten people who were not current clients of Windham Enterprises. "Danetta has set it off up in here."

"And look at all the fine sistahs in here," Kevin said, while ogling a couple of women that passed by.

"You behave," Marshall told him. "I'm going to go find Danetta." Marshall turned away from Kevin on his way over to the display table to ask if anyone had seen Danetta when Kevin tapped him on the shoulder. "Man, I don't have time for you and all your drooling. I've got business to take care of."

Kevin tapped his shoulder again and said, "I think I found Danetta."

Marshall turned back around. "Where?"

Kevin pointed toward the dance floor. Marshall looked, but didn't see Danetta. So he asked again, "Where?"

"Man, open your eyes. She's right there, shaking her moneymaker with that short rainbow swirly dress on."

Short wasn't the word for the dress the woman at the edge of the dance floor had on. The woman was jiggling and wiggling in ways that made Marshall want to snatch her dance partner off the floor so that he could make a move on that disco goddess. The woman on that dance floor was not Danetta. He was about to tell Kevin as much, but just then, another man whispered in the woman's ear and she turned away from the guy she'd been dancing with in order to dance with the new guy.

As the woman turned and gave Marshall a clear view of her face, he sucked in his breath. He'd never expected to see his

Danetta in something so risqué. If she did so much as a half bend, he and everyone else would be able to see all of her glory.

"Man, Danetta is hot," Kevin said.

"Used To Be My Girl" by the O'Jays started playing. Marshall saw the way Kevin was looking at Danetta. He glanced back at the dance floor and noticed how the two men Danetta was dancing with were ogling her. He strutted toward the dance floor with one thought in mind: he needed to rescue *his* girl from all of these wild-eyed men.

CHAPTER 7

Marshall's blood was boiling as he marched over to the dance floor. Danetta was dancing, laughing and having the time of her life. But as she turned from one man to the next, Marshall saw the way the man dancing behind her would stare at her backside, and he didn't like that one bit. Nobody was going to treat his girl like a piece of meat.

As he stepped on the dance floor the lyrics "used to be my girl" blared through the speakers. Marshall used to love that song, but as he tapped Danetta on the shoulder, he wondered if those lyrics might be telling him something . . . like that this was a new Danetta, bouncing around on the dance floor, looking all good in a dress so short that it must have been bought in the girls' department. Danetta was no longer *his girl.*

"Hey you, you're late," Danetta said as she turned toward Marshall, grinning like she knew she was the queen of this prom.

"I had to pick up Super Fly," Marshall said while pointing at Kevin and wishing he had on a jacket, so he could take it off and cover her up with it.

Danetta took one look at Kevin and burst out laughing. "Why did you let that fool come here dressed like that?"

"You know I can't control Kevin." Danetta was still dancing as she talked to Marshall. He put his hand in hers and began walking her off the dance floor.

"Hey," one of the men protested.

"Sorry," Marshall said without looking back. "We have some business to discuss."

"The song isn't over yet," Danetta said.

"Don't worry about the song; I just want to talk to you for a second." *Used to be my girl* . . .

"What are you up to, Marshall?"

Most of the round tables seated eight people, but there were a few tall, round tables throughout the room that only had two tall chairs with them. This type of seating was meant more for one-on-one communications. If clients or anyone else wanted to have a semiprivate conversation during the party, he or Danetta would always walk them over to one of the taller tables. That's where Marshall took Danetta now.

Once they were seated at the table, Marshall moved the vase of multicolored flowers to the side. Then he remembered how mad Danetta had gotten about receiving his single red rose, and at that moment with her sitting there looking all good, Marshall wanted nothing more than to please her. He pulled the half dozen roses out of the vase, wiped some of the water off with the napkins that had been placed on the table and handed them to Danetta. "Happy Valentine's Day, boo," he said with a smile.

She took the roses out of his hand and then hit him upside the head with them. "I oughta boo you. How you gon' give me flowers that have been sitting on any random table and then have the nerve to say, 'Happy Valentine's Day'? And anyway, Valentine's Day was two days ago."

"Hey, I bought the flowers that are on all these tables."

"Windham Enterprises bought the flowers," Danetta countered.

"I am Windham Enterprises, so what's the difference?" Marshall was truly clueless about Danetta's response. If he had brought a date to this event and handed her the roses out of the vase, his date would have smiled and thanked him for being so sweet, but not Danetta.

"No, you are Marshall Windham. Windham Enterprises is a company. Corporations aren't people, my friend," Danetta singsonged her backward imitation of a silly remark Mitt Romney said while campaigning for the presidency.

He'd handed her the flowers as an icebreaker. She'd been mad at him lately and he had just wanted to see her smile at him again like she used to. But now he didn't know what to do, so he changed the subject. "I guess you were right about having Ryla plan the party for us again this year. Our guests seem to be having a good time." He squinted his eyes at her as he added, "It looked like you were having a good time, too."

"I am thoroughly enjoying myself. And I have you to thank for that."

Uh-uh, he wasn't about to take credit for the way she was flaunting herself in front of all of these men. "Don't thank me, you and Ryla planned most of this event."

"Yeah, but you're the one who suggested that we do it up old-school style."

That was when I thought you'd be wearing that '70s flower child dress, he thought but said, "Yeah, but look at you . . . I never thought you'd wear a girl's shirt to one of our parties."

"Me? Look at you," she said with a bit of indignation.

"What's wrong with what I have on?" He looked down at his clothes. "It's perfectly respectable."

"I guess so, if you're Mr. T." Danetta shook her head, as she asked, "Why on earth do you have ten pounds of silver around your neck?"

Marshall looked down at the dollar-sign medallion around his neck. In truth, he'd forgotten that he put the thing on. He took the chain from around his neck and placed it on the table. "This was part of Kevin's mack daddy look. I put it on as a joke. I forgot to take it off before we stepped onto the boat."

"Thank God that was just a joke. I was getting worried about you, for a minute there." She smiled and it seemed for the first time, Marshall realized what a beautiful smile she had.

"What about you," Marshall said as he eyed her from head to toe and back again. "Coming in here in your go-go boots and your . . . shirt. Showing our clients everything your mama gave you."

"There's nothing wrong with what I have on."

Sulking, Marshall said, "You told me you

were going to wear that long dress you had on at that costume party we went to a few years back."

"Yeah so, I changed my mind. What's the big deal?"

"Love Train" by the O'Jays started playing. Ryla began hustling everyone into a Soul Train dance line. Danetta popped up out of her seat and headed for the dance floor. Marshall grabbed her arm. "Hey, what's the rush? We were talking."

"I know Marshall, but I love this song and they're doing a dance line. Just meet me on the stage in a few minutes for the presentation." With that, Danetta was back on the dance floor. Marshall began rubbing his temple as he once again caught several brothers with their eyes on her. He was ticked off that Danetta would wear an outfit like that to a company event. But the thing that bothered Marshall most was that he couldn't figure out whether he was ticked because of the attention she was getting at a company event, or because of the fact that she was getting the attention, period.

When the Soul Train line stopped Marshall found himself in the back of the room, watching as Danetta walked onto the stage with an oversized ten thousand dollar check in her hands. He was supposed to be on the stage with her, but he was afraid of what he would do standing next to her with their clients and friends watching.

So, he stayed in the background, admiring this beautiful, creative and brilliant woman who was so caring that she had the foresight to turn their business party into a fundraiser, just so she could give back to the community.

"What's up Marshall's butt?" Surry asked as she came off the dance floor with her latest dance partner and stood next to Ryla and Danetta.

"What are you talking about?" Danetta asked.

"He's been frowning ever since he got here. And I've noticed him watching you like a hawk," Surry said.

"Now that you mention it, I've noticed Marshall's bad mood, also," Ryla said.

Rolling her eyes heavenward, Danetta said, "He's mad because I've been dancing, so he's had to man the product table, I guess. I'm normally the one manning the table while he dances with his date and networks with our current clients."

"That doesn't sound like Marshall . . . to be mad about doing a little work," Ryla said.

"He didn't even help me give the money we raised to Destiny Home for Girls."

Danetta shrugged as if it didn't matter. "Maybe he's busy chasing behind some woman."

Surry said, "I don't think he brought a date with him this year. At least I haven't seen a woman around him that looks as if she was trying to mark her territory, like his women normally act."

Danetta was shocked by that revelation. Marshall always had a woman dangling on his arm. She had never dreamed that Marshall would show up empty-handed. That's why she had almost asked Mark, the guy she'd gone to lunch with a couple of days ago, to attend this event with her. But by the end of the date, when she'd ended up paying for lunch before Mark had the audacity to ask her for gas money, she knew he wasn't the one.

When she noticed Marshall standing by the product table, she told her friends, "Let me go over there and check on Marshall." She walked over to Marshall she asked, "How is business?" When she really wanted to ask, *How come no date?*

"Business is good. I've talked us up to a few interested people, handed out some brochures and even managed to eat a couple of roast beef sandwiches in the process."

"Busy man." As she said this, she put her

hands behind her back and eyed the product table, because looking at Marshall was causing all sorts of thoughts to roam through her mind. He was standing there looking so fine, that she wanted to lay hands on him in the worst kind of way. She took a deep breath and as she turned back to him, her mind was back on business. "Look, if you want to go and enjoy the party, I can stay here and talk to anyone wandering around our product table."

He put his hands in his pockets. "Naw, you go ahead and enjoy yourself. I'm going to do some more mingling in a minute." He picked up the brochures and told her, "Anyone interested in our company can read about us in this pamphlet. No reason for you to be stuck at this table."

"Papa's Got a Brand New Bag" burst through the speakers and a wide smile spread across Danetta's face. "All right, you convinced me, Marshall. I'm going back to the dance floor. I'll talk to you later."

"Okay, hon, enjoy yourself." *But not too much.*

Popping her fingers, Danetta headed back to her girlfriends. She was hoping that Ryla and Surry would go onto the dance floor with her. They were grown women now, and no longer had to worry about teenage boys making snide remarks about girls dancing together because they couldn't get a guy to dance with them. Unfortunately, Ryla and Surry were already on the dance floor while she was left without a partner. Just as she was thinking about dragging Marshall onto the dance floor, someone whispered in her ear.

"Waiting for someone?"

Danetta swirled around to see the face that belonged to the baritone voice that had just whispered in her ear. And all she could think as she stood staring was *OMG,* because God must have sent this chocolate delight her way. And she was going to snatch him up before Surry got a good look at him. "I think I was waiting for you," Danetta said, trying to sound as if she had game to match his game.

"Is that a fact?" He smiled, and then asked, "Would you like to dance?"

"Love to." She walked onto the floor with the gentleman and began dancing and having a good time.

When one song ended and another began, her dance partner showed no signs of being tired. He leaned into her and said, "My name is Darnell Hinton. I wanted to thank you for sending an invitation for this event to my company."

"You're welcome. I'm glad you could come. So, is your company interested in doing business with us?"

With a raised eyebrow, Darnell said, "I'm sure we can do a little business, but right now what I'm interested in is something very personal with you."

"Is that right?" Danetta asked, enjoying the game that she and Darnell were playing.

Darnell nodded. "I'd like to take you out to dinner, if that's okay."

Another fast song was playing, so they were a little too close for the dance, but Danetta didn't care. This brother was feeling her and she was definitely feeling him. "Dinner sounds good."

Someone tapped Darnell on the shoulder and asked, "Can I cut in?"

Darnell looked back at Danetta and asked, "Can I get your number?"

"My telephone number is in the brochure on the display table." With that said, Darnell walked off and another man took his place.

"Yo, I'm gon' have to hire Danetta's friend for my birthday bash," Kevin said as he walked over to Marshall carrying a heaping plate of food.

"Yeah, they've done a great job with the

whole event. I just wish I had brought a date. Then I'd be having just as much fun as Danetta is having."

"Don't playa hate. Your girl is working this room, and I say 'bout time."

Was Danetta still his girl? "I'm just tired of all these men trying to push up on her. Danetta isn't used to this type of attention. I just don't want her to get caught up with the wrong somebody, if you know what I mean."

Kevin gave Marshall a look they normally reserved for fake brothers trying to act brand-new when they were yesterday's news. "Mmph, I know what you mean all right."

Before Marshall had time to ask Kevin about his sarcasm, the music changed from fast to slow. He turned toward the dance floor and the sucka that Danetta had been fast dancing with started whispering in her ear. Uh-uh, not on his watch . . . it just really wasn't that type of party. Marshall stalked over to the dance floor, tapped the guy on the shoulder and said, "It's my turn now."

The guy looked at Danetta, hoping she would object, but she smiled sweetly and then turned to Marshall and said, "Are you sure you want to dance to this song?"

As an answer, Marshall took her in his arms, pulled her close, so that they were chest to breast, as they moved to Otis Redding's "I've Been Loving You Too Long." He twirled her around and brought her back to his chest as Otis belted out ". . . can't stop now". Marshall closed his eyes as Danetta rested her head on his shoulder. The music was so intoxicating, it had Marshall rethinking this whole 'friends but not lovers' thing he had going on with Danetta. Dancing with her, having her in his arms felt right to him. At this moment, Marshall wanted to hold Danetta like this forever. He opened his eyes and looked down at her. She smiled up at him and just before he got lost in those beautiful brown eyes of hers, he reminded himself that this was Danetta . . . She was not just his friend, but the only friendly relationship he had with a woman not in his family. Did he really want to mess that up?

Before he could answer his own question the music changed and some guy was tapping him on the shoulder. He didn't mind relinquishing the dance because the DJ was now playing "I Heard It Through the Grapevine" and no one was slow dancing anymore.

But as he moved away from the dance

floor and turned back to see Danetta smiling at the man who'd taken his place, he realized that he didn't need the grapevine. He was seeing it with his own two eyes. He was losing his best girl, and he desperately wanted to turn back the hands of time.

CHAPTER 8

"Excuse me, aren't you Marshall Windham?" A well-groomed man with pink roses in his hands asked as he looked around the building with confusion etched across his face.

Marshall stopped in front of the man who, despite obviously being lost, had a confident air about him. He looked like the kind of guy Marshall would hang out with. "The one and only," Marshall said.

"Thank God, I think I've gotten turned around in this building."

"What can I help you find?"

"I'm trying to find someone who works at Windham Enterprises. The security guard isn't at the desk and the information board next to the elevator shows that Windham Enterprises is on the fourth and fifth floors."

"We share this building with four other companies. Who are you looking for?"

"Danetta Harris."

The pink roses in the man's hand told Marshall that this visit had nothing to do with Windham business. "Danetta works on the same floor I do. I'll take you to her." Marshall hit the up button for the elevator and waited.

"So, how long have you and Danetta worked together?"

"Danetta and I have been *partners* for seven years." Marshall said the word 'partners' with extra emphasis and deliberately left out the fact that they were partners in business only. Marshall didn't know why he'd done that, except that something about this guy, with his confident swag and flowers in hand, bugged him.

The man pulled a business card out of his jacket pocket and handed it to Marshall. "My name is Darnell Hinton. I'm Vice President of Sales at Paper Works. So, if you don't have a company handling your paper products such as business cards, invoices, envelopes and such, I could set up some time to go over our product line."

Marshall stuck out his hand. The lost boy with the expensive suit shook it. "Nice to meet you." They stepped into the elevator; Marshall took the card and then asked, "How do you know Danetta?"

"I'm taking her to dinner tonight. I just

wanted to stop by this morning and give her these flowers."

He could only hope that Danetta would knock him over the head with those lame pink roses. "Is it a blind date or something?"

"Not really. I did see her profile on Black PeopleMeet.com and was going to introduce myself through that dating service, but then I received an invitation to the Valentine's Day party you threw last week. I decided to attend and we hooked up there."

The elevator stopped and the door opened. Marshall was too stunned to move. Danetta had gone out on a lunch date last week with some dude she'd met on Facebook, she'd signed up for some internet dating service and now she was making dates at their business functions, even though she acted as if he'd committed a carnal sin whenever he tried to mix a little pleasure with business. He didn't want to say that Danetta was a hypocrite, but he was sure thinking it.

"Is this our floor?" Darnell asked.

Snapping out of his trance, Marshall stepped off the elevator. "Let me show you to Danetta's office." As they walked down the hall, Marshall glanced at Darnell. The brother didn't look like the type of guy who had to pay dating services to get a woman.

That thought caused him to worry that Danetta might be hooking up with some Jack the Ripper . . . meeting lonely women online so he could take them back to his place and slice them up. He might even be a Jeffrey Dahmer who likes dark meat. "What gives, man, why are you looking for women online? Seems to me a guy like you should be able to find a woman with little effort."

"I didn't become vice president of my sales department by chasing the ladies 24-7. I travel a lot and work long hours. The internet just makes dating easier for me."

Okay, Marshall could get with that answer. Neither he nor any of his boys would go lurking around the internet to find a woman, but he wasn't going to throw salt on this man's game. Monica was seated at her desk outside Danetta's office. Marshall handed the man off to her and then told Monica, "Please remind Danetta that we're supposed have drinks with a client at Mc-Cormick & Schmick's tonight." He glanced over at Darnell and then back to Monica. "She evidently has dinner plans, but this client is important."

Monica picked up the phone and dialed into Danetta's office. After a pause, she said, "A Darnell Hinton is here to see you."

Darnell turned to Marshall and said, "I love that restaurant. I can cancel our reservations and make dinner reservations at McCormick's."

With a raised eyebrow, Marshall asked, "You'd do that?"

He nudged Marshall with his elbow like they were conspirators of the same game. "Yeah, man. There may come a time when I need to mix a little business with pleasure. She can't complain if I let her do it first."

This guy was a real romantic; no wonder he had to prowl the internet to find a woman.

Danetta opened her door and walked out of her office. She was wearing a pantsuit today. But it wasn't like the pantsuits she used to wear . . . with the long jackets hanging well below her backside. No, this suit jacket cut off just above where her extremely formfitting pants began. The suit didn't hide one bump or curve. The woman had been holding out on him all these years. Never once had she worn anything that made him believe that she was rocking an hourglass body like the one she obviously had.

Darnell stepped forward, grinning from ear to ear. Marshall wanted to trip the man, take those flowers out of his hand and give them to Danetta himself. When Danetta started grinning at her internet-lover, Marshall had witnessed all he could stand. He turned and walked back to his office and slammed the door shut.

"Thanks for agreeing to have dinner here, Darnell. I really appreciate that you were okay with my meeting with some clients for a few minutes."

"It wasn't a problem at all. I have my BlackBerry with me, so I got a little work done while you networked with your clients."

Danetta was really feeling this guy. He was cool about the demands of her job when most men would feel neglected by a woman trying to take care of her business and her man, too. He also brought her flowers at work for everyone to see — that was the first time something like that had ever happened to her. She was in no way counting that single rose Marshall sent her every year. Everyone in the office knew it was nothing more than a friendship rose. And she certainly wasn't thinking about those roses Marshall tried to give her at the Valentine's party. Thank God Darnell had some sense. He was professional, kind and, judging by the flowers he brought her, Danetta thought that Darnell could probably be quite romantic.

"Are you ready to order dinner, or do you think you'll need to go back over there?" He pointed at the table where Marshall sat with two other men and a woman whose eyes had been glued on Marshall the entire time Danetta sat with them.

Danetta turned toward the table. She watched Marshall hold court for a moment and then turned back to her date. "No, Marshall has it under control."

"All right then, let's get our party started." He lifted his hand signaling the waiter. They placed their orders and then he said, "I have been waiting for this date ever since our dance the other night."

"Well, thanks for asking me to dance." Danetta batted her eyes, enjoying the flirt game they had going on.

He reached across the table and put her hand in his. Rubbing the back of her hand with his thumb, he asked, "So, are you looking for a serious relationship or just something casual?"

She pulled her hand away and leaned back in her seat a bit. For some reason, she got the distinct impression that Darnell was hoping she'd say that she wanted a casual relationship. He probably was hoping that she'd say something like, just take me to the hotel, have your way with me and then call me when you get time. Not.

"I'm interested in developing a serious relationship." She was actually interested in marriage, but why scare him off on the first date?

He leaned back in his seat and studied her for a moment. "You know, you really are a beautiful woman, Danetta."

She blushed.

"Look at you. You're COO of a major corporation and you're blushing because some guy thinks you're beautiful."

She didn't say anything. Danetta had vast business experience and was comfortable in board meetings and corporate settings, but she didn't have a clue about being coy.

"Yeah," Darnell finally said, "I think I'd like getting serious with you."

Danetta smiled. It was nice to be wanted; however, she hadn't yet decided if this was the man she wanted. But, after her last date, Darnell was hitting a home run. "Let's have dinner first; we can worry later about where we want to go from here."

"I like your style." He leaned closer to her, tried to grab her hand again.

Danetta was enjoying the flattery and wanted to give all her attention to Darnell, but her eyes drifted toward Marshall as he stood up, shook the hands of their clients and began walking them out of the restaurant. Trying to get Marshall's image out of her mind, she turned back to Darnell and flirted with her eyes again. But that's when she heard some commotion going on toward the entrance. The waiter was headed for them with the food they'd ordered, but someone else was barreling down on them, and she looked angry.

Darnell's hands flew under the table as the woman approached them. Danetta watched as he fumbled around under the table and then suddenly his hands were back on the table, with an added gold band on his I'm-spoken-for finger.

"Well, isn't this cozy," the woman said as she glared at Darnell and then turned her venom on Danetta. "So, I suppose you spend your free time stealing men, huh?"

"Excuse me?" was the only comeback Danetta could think of.

The woman pulled up a chair and sat down.

The waiter brought the plates to the table, but Darnell waved the man off.

The woman turned to the waiter. "Oh, please give them their plates. And I'd like the most expensive meal on the menu. I don't care what it is, just bring it to me."

With a smirk on his face, the waiter put the salad plates and bread on the table. "One expensive meal coming up," he said as he walked away.

"We just ordered, honey, so your meal should come out with ours," Darnell said as if an angry woman had not just sat down at their table.

The woman rolled her eyes at him and then turned to Danetta and said, "I just want to thank you for this little date or whatever. Because I haven't been on a date with my lousy husband since I married him."

Danetta stood up, finally understanding what was going on. She might be a little slow sometimes, but she wasn't that slow. "Hold up," she began.

"Sorry I'm late, baby. I just couldn't get away any sooner."

Danetta heard Marshall's voice behind her, then she felt his arm around her waist as he pulled her into an embrace and kissed her. The kiss was soft, sweet and quick, but it sent a jolt through Danetta's body and left her speechless.

"Sit back down, baby. We can handle this bit of business and then be on our way. Did you order me anything to eat?"

Danetta fell back into her seat, eyes on Marshall, not understanding the game he was playing.

"You didn't order for me?" Marshall continued when Danetta didn't respond. He put his hand over hers and said, "That's fine, I don't think this meeting will last that long anyway."

"What meeting?" the woman asked.

Marshall ignored her and turned to Darnell. "Look Mr. Hinton, we might as well cut to the chase. I reviewed your proposal, but we're just not interested in what you're selling."

"This is a business meeting." The woman clasped her hands over her mouth as she looked from Danetta and then back to her husband. "Oh my God, I'm so embarrassed."

"Don't worry about it, Mavis." The same hand Darnell had used to caress Danetta's hand, he now used to caress his wife's. "It was an easy mistake."

"I was confused because of the way she was looking at you when I walked in." Mavis pointed at Danetta. "She didn't seem like she was interested in just business."

Darnell tsk-tsked and shook his head, as if to say, poor him, he was always having to fend off women and their advances. "I didn't pay it any attention. You know how some of these women are."

"Now just wait a minute," Danetta said, beginning to rise from her seat again.

Marshall gripped her hand tighter. Danetta got the message and kept her seat. She looked into Marshall's eyes and saw that he was ready to let this jerk get away with his charade. She was about to snatch her hand from his, but Marshall gripped her hand tighter.

He stood up and said, "Well, I hope you and your wife enjoy your dinner." Pulling Danetta with him as he continued holding on to her hand. "We've got to go, because I am taking my baby dancing."

The waiter came back to the table with the food. Marshall told him, "Put hers in a to-go bag. We'll pick it up at the hostess desk." He then walked Danetta away from the table and stood at the front waiting for her food to be brought to them.

"Why didn't you let me tell him off?" Danetta fumed.

"Because I didn't want you to have to deal with his wife. That woman looked like she came in here to fight."

Danetta looked back at the table. The woman had about thirty pounds on her, and Danetta wasn't sure she would have been able to win that fight. She turned back to Marshall. "Thank you, Marshall. I don't know what I would have done if you hadn't come over there," Danetta whispered as she grabbed her to-go bag from the waiter.

As they walked outside, Marshall said, "Don't worry about it, I'm happy to be your knight in shining armor any time you need me."

She nudged him with her shoulder. "It's always nice to have a knight at my disposal."

"But Danetta, for real, you are a beautiful woman, why on earth are you trolling the internet looking for men?"

"What are you talking about? I didn't meet Darnell online."

"Darnell said that he saw your profile on BlackPeopleMeet.com. Why would you sign up for some internet dating service?"

Because you don't want me, she wanted to scream at him. But instead she just lifted a hand and said, "Not right now, Marshall, okay?"

Her pride had taken a beating with ol' flower-toting Darnell. She didn't need a lecture right then. She needed a friend. He put an arm around her waist and walked her to his SUV. "All right, come on woman, let's go."

"Where?"

"I'm taking you dancing, just like I told Darnell and the Mrs. Now, get in the car and let me make a quick call to reserve our table."

CHAPTER 9

He took her to Sullivan's Steakhouse. Marshall ordered the lamb chops with asparagus and white cheddar au gratin potatoes. While Danetta ordered the pan-seared sea bass "Hong Kong style" with three cheese mac with garlic butter crust and sautéed green beans. Marshall and Danetta savored each mouthwatering morsel as they listened to the soulful, uplifting sounds of the live jazz band.

"Are you enjoying yourself?" Marshall asked.

Danetta picked up her napkin and dabbed around the corners of her mouth as she glanced around the restaurant. She had never dined at Sullivan's, but was loving the ambiance . . . the dimmed lights, black tablecloth with the glowing candle. Her fantasy about having a candlelit dinner with Marshall was coming true. Although she was sure Marshall hadn't intended to bring her to such a romantic place. "I am enjoying myself. I love jazz bands. But I thought you were taking me dancing?" she needled him.

"Oh baby, if it's dancing you want, then that's what you'll get." He held out a hand for her as he stood up.

Danetta shook her head. "Nobody else is dancing. Everybody is just sitting and listening."

"We don't have to be like them. Come on, let your hair down."

She gave him a sorrowful look as she said, "The last time I let my hair down, some man's wife was about ready to pull it out."

"You know that I wouldn't have let that happen."

Nodding with assurance, she said, "I know that. But I still don't want to dance. I really don't like for people to stare at me."

Marshall sat back down. He put Danetta's hand in his and waited until she looked him in the eyes. "You're beautiful, Danetta. Why are you so afraid to let people see that?"

Was she afraid? "I don't know. My aunt always told me that beauty is from the inside out. So, I've never really worried much about how I looked on the outside until recently."

"Yeah, well, I normally agree with most

116

things Auntie Sarah says, but people see the outside before they ever figure out what kind of a person you are. So, it's best to let a man see what you're working with right up front."

"Did I miss something? What are you talking about?"

"I'm talking about you . . . that dress . . . your hair." He stared at her lips as if he wanted to kiss them as he said, "And this new lipstick you're wearing. You look good, Danetta. I just don't understand why you've been hiding your true self for so long."

Marshall was still holding her hand and Danetta was speechless. It felt so good being with him like this. She wondered if he could feel what she felt, but she didn't dare ask. Marshall had never said anything like what he'd just said to her before. She just couldn't find words to respond.

A waiter came to their table carrying a dozen long-stemmed red roses. He had a wide grin on his face as he told Danetta, "I was told to bring these roses to the loveliest lady in the room."

Danetta looked around as if the waiter had somehow slipped up and walked over to the wrong table.

"He's talking about you, D," Marshall told her before she managed to direct the man to another table.

Danetta reached out and grabbed the roses as her eyes widened with the revelation. "You got me roses . . . a whole dozen?"

"Since you're obviously the loveliest woman in this restaurant, I must confess that I felt compelled to buy you some roses."

"But when did you do it? I don't understand . . . I rode here with you and I never heard you say anything about flowers to the waiter." Danetta was practically giddy. Tomorrow morning, she was going to throw those tired old pink roses Darnell brought her in the trash and replace them with her beautiful red roses.

With a devilish glint in his eyes, Marshall said, "I ordered them before I joined you in the car, while I was reserving our table."

"Thank you, Marshall, you can't even imagine how much I needed these flowers right now."

"You're welcome . . . and maybe the next time I hand you flowers off a table, you won't feel the need to hit me over the head with them."

Looking a bit embarrassed, Danetta said, "I'm sorry about that, Marshall. I should have been gracious enough to accept those flowers just as I'm accepting these now."

He stood up and held his hand out to her.

"I'll forgive you if you dance with me."

Danetta glanced around the room. Everyone appeared to be having a good time, eating and listening to the soulful jazz music. She didn't feel like being a party pooper, so she grabbed Marshall's hand and allowed him to take her onto the dance floor.

They moved in a syncopated rhythm, from side to side, back and forth. Then Marshall twirled her around and slowed the dance down. "Marshall, people are staring at us," she said as their bodies collided together.

He looked down at her with adoration showing in his eyes. "Of course they're staring. Did you forget that you're the loveliest woman in the room?"

Grinning from ear to ear, Danetta said, "Marshall Windham, sometimes, you say the darndest things."

His words relaxed Danetta. She put her head on Marshall's shoulder and allowed the music to lull her into a dream state as they continued to slow dance across the floor. They danced through three songs and then sat back down and ordered chocolate cake. The two were feeling good as they walked out of the restaurant and got in the car.

As Marshall held Danetta's door for her, he said, "Thanks for going out with me, D,

I really had a good time with you tonight."

"I bet you say that to Veronica and all the other girls," Danetta said, trying to make light of his comment.

Marshall shivered. "Please don't mention that woman to me."

"Why, what's wrong with her? A couple of weeks ago, you were upset about not being able to take her on your business trip, now you don't even want to hear her name . . . I swear I don't understand men."

"D, it's not even like that. That woman is crazy. I had to get a restraining order on her."

Danetta's mouth hung open. "What?"

"She scratched my car and flattened my tires after I told her I wasn't taking her out of town with me. So, really, it's all your fault."

She playfully shoved his shoulder. "Shut up."

Laughing, Marshall said, "Oh, so you don't want to take responsibility for the drama you caused, huh?"

Danetta shook her head in disbelief. "I just can't believe you had to get a restraining order on Veronica. I've never known you to date crazy women before."

"Well, don't be too hard on her. If you had somebody putting it down right, you'd lose your mind when it was over, too."

"Ha," Danetta laughed at Marshall's comment, and then declared, "I certainly wouldn't lose my mind over some 'love 'em and leave 'em' hound dog who thinks he's something because he's talented in the bedroom."

"You just haven't had the right hound dog," Marshall said with a devilish grin.

"I don't want a hound dog at all. I'm not into hookups and then cross my fingers and hope that he'll call me in the morning stuff."

"So, again, I ask what are you doing trolling the internet? Because you know those guys only want one thing."

"Don't all men just want one thing?"

"Not all men." He took his eyes off the road and glanced over at Danetta. "Variety is the spice of life, D. Sometimes a man just wants a woman he can talk to."

"I still can't believe that you got a restraining order against her. That just doesn't seem like something you would do."

"Danetta, I'm telling you, that woman is coo-coo for Cocoa Puffs. When she came over to my house the day I had to leave for that business trip, I thought she was going to knife me or something. But instead of that, she broke the ceramic lamp that you bought me for my thirtieth birthday and then she keyed my SUV."

"What?" Her mouth hung open for a moment. "You didn't tell me that she broke the lamp I bought you." Shaking her head, she continued, "I only remember seeing her at the office once, but I would have never thought that she was that type of woman."

"You and me both. I normally take applications before I start dating a woman . . . you know, find out if she has any mental health issues or if she likes playing with knives after an argument with her man . . . things like that. But Veronica looked so much like you, I naturally thought she'd be cool people."

Did Marshall just say that he dated a woman because she reminded him of her? What does that mean? "What are you talking about, Marshall? Veronica and I don't look alike. That woman is the flashy, model type you normally date; I'm nothing like that."

He pulled up in front of her house and turned off the car. Marshall turned to Danetta and let his eyes roam the length of her. When he met her eyes again he said, "You look pretty flashy to me."

"With the way you're looking at me, you'd think I was at the Super Bowl and Justin Timberlake was exposing my breast to the world or something."

"Well, you are definitely bringing sexy back."

The silence was thick in the car as their eyes met and locked. Marshall had this look of surprise on his face, like he'd been caught off guard, and couldn't quite get his bearings. Then they started leaning toward each other. They were about to kiss. Danetta didn't know if this was such a good idea, but she couldn't stop herself. The kiss he'd given her at dinner tonight was closed-mouthed; Danetta desperately wanted to know what an opened-mouth, tongues twirling, passionate kiss with this man would feel like.

She'd dreamed about kissing him since the day they met. But never in a million years did she ever think Marshall would look at her the way he was looking at her right now or that he would . . .

Marshall's lips touched hers and all thought ceased. There was only the heat that radiated between them as his mouth devoured hers. Danetta scooted over, moving closer to the fire. She lifted her hands to wrap them around Marshall. But someone tapped on her window causing Danetta to jump.

Marshall ran his hand through his low-cut hair. As he pulled away from Danetta he turned a smile toward the person knocking at her window.

She turned her head and saw her Aunt Sarah standing outside the car. And that's when it hit her — this was Thursday night. She normally hung out with her aunt on Thursday evenings. She'd forgotten to call and tell her aunt that she had a date. And now her aunt had caught her kissing Marshall. She opened the passenger door and said, "Aunt Sarah, I'm so sorry; I forgot all about you tonight."

"I cooked dinner and left it in the house. I was just getting ready to leave when you and Marshall pulled up." She leaned down and waved at Marshall. "How are you doing, Marshall?"

He gave a charming smile. "Doing well, Aunt Sarah."

Danetta got out of the car.

"So were you and Marshall on a date?"

"No, Auntie, we were not on a date," Danetta said with obvious irritation in her voice.

"I didn't mean to pry, dear, it's just that you look so pretty and you were just kissing Marshall, weren't you?"

Marshall yelled from the car, "She *was* on a date, Aunt Sarah."

Danetta turned back and glared at Marshall. How dare he sell her out like that?

Aunt Sarah looked from Marshall to Danetta. She then turned back to Marshall and said, "Get on out of that car and come in the house so we can talk."

Danetta held up her hand and confessed, "All right, all right, if you must know, I was on a date tonight."

"Oh that's wonderful. Now you and Marshall come on in the house and tell me all about it."

"Not much to tell," Danetta said as Marshall rolled up the window and got out of the car. "I met this guy. We went out to dinner and then his wife showed up."

CHAPTER 10

When Marshall told Aunt Sarah that Danetta had been on a date, he hadn't been referring to the time she'd spent with Darnell and his wife. He'd been talking about the time they'd spent at dinner and dancing. But since she went there, Marshall decided to go with the flow as he walked into the house with Danetta and Aunt Sarah.

Danetta continued her story. "It was awful, Auntie. I thought this guy was perfect; I'm just thankful that Marshall was at the restaurant with us. He saved me from looking like a total fool."

"Where'd you meet this guy?" Her aunt sounded concerned.

"He attended our annual dinner party."

"Yeah, but Aunt Sarah, this man first saw her on some internet dating site."

Danetta poked Marshall with her elbow.

"Is that true, honey? Are you dating men

off the internet?" Aunt Sarah asked with wide-eyed terror.

"It's no big deal, Auntie, I just joined this matchmaking service. I haven't even accepted any dates from the site yet. Marshall is just running his mouth."

Aunt Sarah sat down on the couch and shook her head.

"What?"

Aunt Sarah looked at her niece and boldly said, "I told you before, Danetta, that my Bible says, 'the man who finds a wife finds a good thing and then he obtains favor from God.' "

Danetta rolled her eyes, because she'd heard this speech too many times to count.

Marshall chimed in. "I don't know about whether or not the man has to find the woman, but I do think Danetta has lost her mind with this internet dating stuff."

Aunt Sarah shook her head. "All I know is, if you're out there trying to find a man, rather than waiting on him to find you, you're just going to keep running into the same type of messy situations as you got yourself involved in tonight."

She had run into her share of messy situations these past few weeks. But she wasn't about to tell her aunt about that. "Aunt Sarah, please calm down. It is perfectly all right in this day and age for a woman to ask a man out. Right, Marshall?"

Marshall shook his head. "Don't look at me. I don't want no part of this. Like Aunt Sarah said, this whole thing is just messy."

"Thanks, Marshall."

He hit his chest with his fist. "Hey, I'm here for you."

Aunt Sarah put her head in her hands as she shook it. When she faced her niece again, she said, "Right before your mama went home, I promised her that I would look after you."

Danetta cringed at those words. Her aunt Sarah always said that her mom 'went home' as if she was just down the street and around the corner, and Danetta could go visit her whenever she felt like it. But in truth her mom was buried six feet deep in the cemetery where all of her other dead relatives were buried. Pauline Harris died before her only child graduated from high school.

During her mother's brief illness, Danetta fully expected her mother to recover. She was young and her aunt Sarah had filled her head with the knowledge of a loving God. Since God was so loving, Danetta knew that He would never allow her mother to die while she was still so young. But He had, and that one cruel act solidified things for her.

"Maybe if you start wearing your promise ring again, that will help you to wait on the right man to come along."

"I hate to break it to you, Aunt Sarah, but I took that promise ring off the day I lost my virginity to a guy I'd only known for two weeks."

Marshall sucked in a breath and clamped his hand over his mouth as if he couldn't believe women did things like that. "How you gon' tell Aunt Sarah something like that?"

Sarah waved off Marshall's concern as she responded to her niece. "I knew why you took the ring off. I'm just saying that if you put it back on, maybe you'll start to remember why you wore it in the first place."

If her aunt wasn't so serious, the very idea would be laughable. You couldn't put the genie back in the bottle and become a virgin again. She'd put that promise ring on when she was fifteen and eager to pledge that she would keep her virginity until she married. But when her mother died, suddenly nothing seemed to matter anymore.

She'd stopped caring about what God thought was best and began living life on her own terms. She wasn't thinking about any purity promise ring or about God and the so-called man He could bring into her life. Her own father hadn't wanted to be a part of her life. He'd remarried and wanted nothing to do with the child from his first marriage. So, with the help of her aunt, she had taken care of herself since she was seventeen. So, Danetta was quite capable of finding her *own* good thing, thank you very much.

"Well, just think about what I said, okay?"

"Why are you rubbing your arm like that?"

Sarah looked down. She hadn't noticed that she was rubbing her arm, *but now that Danetta mentioned it . . .* "It's been going numb on me."

Danetta rolled her eyes. Her aunt took care of everybody else, but neglected herself as if she were superhuman. "When's the last time you had a checkup?"

She shook her head. "I know what you're going to say, and I don't want you to worry about me. I've been busy with all of my volunteer work, but I promise I'll make a doctor's appointment."

Danetta sat down next to her beloved aunt and put her arm around the woman. "See that you do. You're all the family I have left, so I need you in my life."

"That's right, Aunt Sarah," Marshall said.

"You lie down and get some rest; I'll deal with Danetta and her little dating problem." He grabbed Danetta's hand and they walked out of the living room.

In the kitchen, Danetta put her hands on her hips. "You'll deal with me, huh?"

"Look, I'm just trying to help."

"How is that?"

"To stop you from doing all this internet dating, maybe I'll take you out." He took a loose strand of hair and put it behind her ear. He lightly touched his lips to hers and then pulled back. "What do you say? . . . Wanna go out with me?"

She was absolutely appalled. First her aunt tells her she should wait on God to send her a mate . . . then Mr. I-Think-I'm-God, offers her a pity date. "Go home, Marshall. I don't need your help."

"Kevin, open up!" Marshall banged on his friend's door like he was the owner of the property and his bum of a tenant owed him rent money. "Come on, man, I need to talk to you."

"Who's there?" a voice called from inside.

"It's me, Marshall. Open the door."

Kevin opened the door and stepped back as Marshall rushed in. "What's up, man? Is the police after you or what?"

"I kissed Danetta. I can't believe I did that." Marshall moved back and forth while rubbing his temples. He didn't understand what was happening to him or why he was feeling these emotions about Danetta.

"What are you talking about?"

"She's just so sexy," he continued. "I can't get her out of my head. And I'm so jealous of the men she's been going out with."

"Who is sexy? And who are you jealous of?"

Marshall stopped in his tracks. He stared at Kevin for a moment. "Haven't you been listening to me? I'm talking about Danetta."

"Danetta who?" Kevin asked.

"Boy, are you dense or what? You know what Danetta I'm talking about . . . my business partner."

"Whoa, wait a minute." He held up his hands. "Are we talking about Danetta Harris? The woman you told me, from your own mouth, that you were just friends with and would never even entertain developing a relationship with?"

"Yeah, but she's driving me crazy with this new attitude she's developed. You saw her at the party."

"Yeah, and baby got back, and curves and bumps . . . I wanted to ask her out myself," Kevin said.

"See what I mean? But it's not just how sexy she is. I can really talk to Danetta. We have history and I'm comfortable with her." Marshall was exasperated. "Now what am I supposed to do?"

Kevin shrugged. "Holler at her. She probably made all those changes to get your attention, anyway."

"I can't just start seeing her. Danetta and I have been friends for ten years and business partners for seven. I can't jeopardize our relationship." Marshall walked into the living room and sat down on the couch. "And anyway, she turned me down when I asked her out."

Kevin laughed as he followed Marshall into the living room. "Say what the what?"

"You heard right. But that wasn't even the worst part of it. Because I really wanted her to say yes." Marshall shook his head. "I don't know what I was thinking."

"Look, man," Kevin said reasonably. "You've been content to bounce from one woman to the next for as long as I've known you. But maybe you're ready to settle down now and maybe that's why you've started seeing Danetta differently."

Marshall stood back up. "I value Danetta as a business partner and a friend. I don't think I could deal with not having her in my life if I tried to have a romantic relationship with her and it blew up." Marshall had never been able to remain friends with any woman he'd ever had a relationship with. He could not even imagine life without Danetta, and didn't want to.

"So, what you're saying, then, is that you'd rather keep Danetta in the friend zone."

Marshall pointed at his friend. "Exactly. And besides, Danetta has changed. She's meeting all these men online and becoming someone I don't even really know."

"Well then, my friend, let's head out to the club tonight. Let's just hang out and have a good time. Maybe you'll meet someone who'll take your mind off Danetta."

Marshall turned up his nose at the thought of stepping foot inside one more booty-call bar. Through the years, he and Kevin had met a lot of women and had some wild times in one nightclub after the next, but Marshall was thirty-two years old now. And he just couldn't deal with one more superficial woman in his life. Not after the incredible moment he shared with Danetta . . . he wanted more. "Maybe some other time, Kevin. I have early meetings tomorrow. I'll just head on home." And he had a lot to think about . . . like the fact that he now wanted more from Danetta than friendship, but for the first time in his life, he was scared to go after what he wanted, for fear of losing his best friend in the process.

CHAPTER 11

"One monkey don't stop no show," Surry said as she, Danetta and Ryla sat in the hair salon waiting to get their do's done.

"What about two clowns? If both show up to the same party, that can stop a show . . . especially if one needs gas money and the other keeps forgetting that he's married," Danetta said.

"Yeah, that wasn't even cool. I wish Marshall had punched that guy in the face, right in front of his wife," Ryla said.

Danetta waved off that suggestion. "Girl please, I wouldn't want Marshall to get into a fight over me."

"I dated this guy once who picked fights with any and every guy who even looked my way. It was kind of cute for about a week, then I was over it," Surry said.

"It takes you about a week or two to get over every man you date," Ryla said with a laugh.

"Well, at least I go out and try to find love," Surry argued. "You won't even give a guy a chance, so don't talk about me, Ryla Evans.

"Hold on, I thought we were talking about my problems. Can we please focus?" Danetta asked.

"Girl, quit crying. You emailed us a picture of this guy you're going to lunch with tomorrow. And let me just say . . . if he has a brother, send him my way," Ryla said while fanning herself with her hand.

Danetta wanted to tell her friends about the kiss she'd shared with Marshall. But she was just too embarrassed to admit that she'd allowed Marshall to lead her around like a cat chasing after a spoil of yarn, only to get to the end of it and find a pity date waiting.

Men were such jerks, Danetta thought as she sat under the dryer fuming. She entered the dating scene again because she wanted a man to call her own. But all she'd found so far was the 'can-I-borrow-some-gas-money?', and the 'oh-did-I-forget-to-mention-I-have-a-wife?' kind of men. The two losers she'd been on dates with were seriously making her reconsider giving guy number three a chance. But since she wasn't about to sit at home and continue dreaming

137

about a man she couldn't have in the way she wanted him, Danetta was not going to let two losers stop her from taking another chance on love.

The sun was out and since it was almost seventy degrees in late February, Danetta decided to walk over to the Chinese restaurant that was across the street from her office complex. Her date was waiting on her and Danetta had motivated herself into high hopes for this new guy. But she wasn't prepared for the piece of eye candy she found herself sitting across the table from. The brother could give Shemar Moore lessons on exploiting his pretty boy face and rock-hard body. "So, Stan." *What was a pretty boy like this doing with a name like Stan?* "What do you do for a living?"

"I'm pretty much a jack-of-all-trades," he said as he slurped his soup as if no one ever taught him proper soup etiquette.

"A jack-of-all-trades, huh? So, what company do you work for?"

He waved off that notion. "I work for myself. I tried working for the man, but it's just too confining for me . . . all of this, 'be on time . . . no, you can't leave early' stuff." He rolled his eyes. "I can't deal with people like that. So, now I get up when I want to and handle the jobs I want to handle." He

138

leaned into her and deepened his voice to the point of seduction as he said, "I'm very good with my hands, you know."

No, no, no, she thought, trying not to let the disappointment settle in. This man was too pretty to be worthless. This was not happening to her.

He leaned back in his seat, grabbed a toothpick off the table and picked his teeth. When he looked back at her, he said, "I bet you have real good health insurance with your company."

Her sandwich was inches away from her mouth. She put it back on her plate. "Excuse me?"

"Aw baby, don't sweat it. You're looking for a man, I get that." His eyes perused her body. "I like what I see, so I'm down with the program, but the woman I hook up with has got to have a good health insurance plan on her job."

She was so tongue-tied that all she could say was a lame, "Excuse me?" again. Then she looked around the restaurant to see if cameramen were about to pop up from somewhere to let her know that she was being punked. She had seen a reality show on television where the guy would pick up a nice-looking woman, and he'd think he'd just hit the jackpot and then she'd come out of her bipolar bag on him. Maybe this guy worked for that dating reality show.

"Don't front, baby girl. You need a man and I need health insurance. I figure we can help each other out."

Her cell phone rang, saving her from having to respond to Mr. I-Want-a-Woman-with-Health-Insurance. Without even looking at the caller ID, she hit talk. "This is Danetta Harris."

"Ms. Harris, this is Ericka Winston at Memorial Hospital. Sarah Davis is in the emergency room and you're listed as her next of kin."

"Oh my God. What happened to her?"

"We'd prefer to discuss this in person. Can you come to the hospital?"

Danetta's hand went to her heart as she shot up from the table. "Is she dead?"

"No, ma'am," the nurse said quickly. "She was alert enough to provide us with your information. But you may want to get here quickly."

She heard the words as if they fell out of her mouth in slow motion. Danetta looked around the restaurant as if someone there could change the reality she was currently dealing with.

"Are you able to come to the hospital?"

Jolted back, she said, "I'm on my way."

She hung up the phone and started walking away from the table, then she remembered that she wasn't alone and turned back to her date. "I have to go."

He stood up. "That phone call sounded serious."

A look of compassion crossed his handsome face and at that moment, Danetta wondered if there was more to Stan than his pretty-boy looks and carefree lifestyle. She didn't have time to explore it, so she shoved the thought aside. "My aunt's in the hospital. I have to go see about her."

"I'm sorry to hear that. Go see about your aunt, I'll take care of things here." He sat back down and waved toward the waiter.

As Danetta rushed to the front of the restaurant tears streamed down her face. She was not prepared for this at all. If Aunt Sarah died, Danetta would be devastated. Danetta's thoughts drifted back to the other night when her aunt complained of numbness in her arm. Why hadn't she taken her to the emergency room right then and there? *Please be okay, Aunt Sarah, just please be okay.*

As she reached out to open the restaurant door, someone touched her shoulder. Danetta thought it was Stan and was a bit annoyed, because he knew that she was in a rush. She brushed the hand off her shoulder and said, "I can't talk now, Stan," and kept walking.

"Danetta, Danetta, it's me." He grabbed her shoulder and turned her around to face him.

"Marshall! What are you doing here?" she asked while wiping the tears from her face.

Looking a bit sheepish, he told her, "I like the food here. Why are you crying? Did that guy do something to upset you?"

Danetta saw the look of cold hard anger on Marshall's face and immediately tried to dispel his anger. "No, my date was okay. It's Aunt Sarah."

"What's wrong with Aunt Sarah?"

Tears broke through once again and ran down her face. "I don't know. I have to get to the hospital." She walked out of the restaurant, headed toward her office building.

Marshall caught up with her. "You're in no condition to drive. Leave your car at work and I'll take you to the hospital."

She glanced at the street. Traffic was heavy. Danetta knew she'd probably have to wait a good five minutes before the light changed so she could cross the street. That was too long to wait. But she didn't want to impose on anyone either. "I can't ask you to do that."

"You didn't." He grabbed her arm and pulled her toward his car. "Stop trying to be superwoman and let me help you."

Grateful for the help, Danetta allowed Marshall to lead her to his car. They sat in silence as Marshall broke the speed limit to get them to the hospital. He pulled up at the emergency-room entrance and Danetta jumped out while he parked the car. The emergency-room doors opened and Danetta rushed in.

She hadn't been in a hospital since her mother died, but as the smell of the place hit her and she scanned the unchanged room, it was as if she were seventeen again. Her mom had been so weak and ill by the time they arrived at the emergency room, that Danetta had had to get a wheelchair and push her up to the admittance window. Her mother had been hooked up to an IV and then wheeled from one testing room to the next. And with one simple word their lives had changed forever . . . cancer.

Pauline Harris hadn't complained about her lot in life, not even when the doctors told her that the cancer had spread throughout her body and there was nothing they could do. All she'd done was ask that they bring another bed into her hospital room.

She wanted to spend her final days with her daughter. And that is what Danetta had done. She spent every single night in that hospital, laughing and joking with her mother. Praying with her, getting her water and ice, and feeding her when Pauline's arms and legs had stopped functioning. Once her mother had passed, Danetta made a vow to never step foot in that hospital ever again. She had kept that vow until today. But she hadn't really broken her vow yet, because Danetta hadn't managed to walk any farther than the entrance of the emergency room before she felt herself hyperventilating.

"Danetta, what's wrong?" Marshall asked as he entered the hospital.

She turned to him, feet still stuck in place. "I can't go in there."

He put his hand on her arm, guiding her forward. "Come on, D, we need to check on Aunt Sarah."

Danetta smiled. From the time she introduced Marshall to her aunt during their college days, Marshall had begun calling her Aunt Sarah — as if she were a part of his family, too. Danetta had met Marshall's family also, but she had never been as comfortable with them as Marshall was with Aunt Sarah. She allowed him to move her over to the admittance window but she couldn't get her thoughts together enough to speak.

"We're here for Sarah Davis," Marshall told the woman behind the glass partition.

She keyed the name into her computer. "She's in bed four," the nurse said as she hit the buzzer for the emergency-room doors.

The doors opened and Marshall ushered Danetta in. Tears flowed down her face as she passed each room. She was thankful that her aunt's room was so close, but that didn't stop her waterfall. They entered the room and Danetta had to put her head between her legs as she tried to breathe again. Marshall rubbed her back and soothingly said, "It's okay, D. Aunt Sarah is right here."

But that was the problem. Her aunt was hooked up to an IV, tubes and wires were all over the place. An oxygen mask was over Aunt Sarah's face. Danetta stood back up. Her aunt's eyes were open. She looked weak, but hadn't died, thank God. Danetta rushed over to the bed and put her hand on her aunt's arm.

Aunt Sarah reached up and tried to wipe the tears away. She pulled the mask from her face, and with a husky voice said, "I'm sorry."

Danetta closed her eyes, willing herself not to be such a baby. When she opened them again, she said, "Don't you worry about me. You just need to concentrate on getting better."

Aunt Sarah looked toward Marshall and said, "T-thanks for being with her."

Marshall stood behind Danetta, putting his hands on her shoulder. "I wouldn't be anywhere else, Aunt Sarah."

Aunt Sarah smiled as she put the oxygen mask back on and closed her eyes.

An orderly stepped into the room. He looked at Sarah and said in a soothing manner, "I'm going to take you for a little ride, okay?"

Aunt Sarah nodded.

"Where are you taking her?" Danetta demanded.

"The doctor ordered a couple of tests."

Danetta knew all about tests and the bad news that came afterward. She marched to the nurse's station and told the woman behind the counter, "I need to speak with my aunt's doctor."

"The patient's name?"

"Sarah Davis, she's in bed four."

The woman reviewed her information and then said, "If you can just have a seat in the waiting area, the doctor will let you know something as soon as we get the test results back."

"I'd rather wait for my aunt in the room."

"That's not possible. The doctor has strict orders for limited visits at this time."

Danetta was getting ready to argue with the woman, but then Marshall put a hand on her shoulder. "Come on, Danetta. I'll sit out there with you."

Marshall's hand was in the small of her back as they walked back into the waiting area. She was a nervous wreck, but with Marshall's reassuring presence, she began to relax.

They sat down and then Marshall asked, "Are you okay, D? I've never seen you so frazzled."

Marshall was used to her take-charge, take-no-prisoners attitude in business, but this was personal. She put her hands in her lap as her shoulders slumped. "I used to live in this hospital."

His brow lifted at that puzzling statement.

"I spent the night here with my mom for about thirty days straight. She died in this hospital."

He pulled her into his arms and held on to her for a long moment. When he let her go, he asked, "Is that why Aunt Sarah apologized to you?"

She nodded. "I haven't been in this hospital since my mom's death. All of that happened thirteen years ago. But when I walked through those doors, I was seventeen all over again. I never thought I'd be back here." His cell phone rang. It was his secretary, Mallory Daniels. He answered and told her to only transfer important calls to his cell phone. For anyone else, he was unavailable.

When he hung up, Danetta said, "You don't have to stay here with me. Go on back to work."

He stared into her eyes. "I'll do no such thing. I'm here as long as you need me."

"I know I seemed like a hysterical fool earlier, but I'm calm now. So, you don't have to worry about me. And anyway, I'm sure you have better things to do than hang around a hospital."

"Do you remember what I told you when you joined me at Windham Enterprises?"

Was he kidding? She remembered almost everything about this man. "You said, 'From now on, it's you and me against the world.' "

His eyes softened as he took her hand in his and leaned back into his seat. "I still feel that way, D. I could no more leave you now than I could forget to breathe."

His eyes were closed as he leaned his head

against the back wall. She took that opportunity to stare at him. Marshall had no idea what his words meant to her. For so long Marshall had only thought of her as a friend, or a little sister . . . but wasn't acting like that now. Could he really want something more from her? Would he ever kiss her again?

He patted her hand. Danetta averted her eyes as he said, "Aunt Sarah is going to be all right. She's got too much life in her to give up now."

Danetta could feel her eyes begin to water again. "Can we talk about something else, please?"

Marshall sat back up in his chair. "Yeah, there is something I wanted to ask you."

"What?" she asked, grateful to be able to think about something else.

"Where'd you meet pretty boy?"

"Who?"

"Don't play dumb. Where did you meet that guy you went out to lunch with today?"

She smiled despite herself. "Oh, Stan."

"Yeah, *Stan*. He said the name as if it left a bad taste in his mouth. "Did you meet that bozo on the internet, too?"

She shrugged. "He emailed me after seeing my photo on a matchmaking website."

"You looked pretty good together when I

saw you at the restaurant."

"Is that why you suddenly decided to have lunch at a Chinese restaurant when you don't even eat Chinese food? Were you spying on me?"

"I like shrimp fried rice."

Giggling for the first time since she'd received the call about her aunt, Danetta said, "You like shrimp fried spying."

"Whatever," Marshall said without confessing to anything. "Just tell me . . . do you like the guy or not?"

"Stan is looking for a woman with —" she did quotation marks with her fingers "— 'health insurance', so he can keep working his flex hours. I don't think things will work out between us."

"He told you that?"

"In so many words."

Marshall laughed.

She shoved him. "It's not funny. I honestly don't know what's wrong with men these days."

"Okay, well I know that Mr. VP of Sales was a loser, but what about the guy who drove the girly car?"

She rolled her eyes. "He asked me for gas money."

Marshall erupted into laughter again. He held his sides as he almost rolled out of his seat. "I knew it. He borrowed that car from his mama and didn't even have enough gas money to get it back to her. You should have told that fool that walking is free and let him hit Hushpuppy Highway." After saying this, he shook from the giggles once again.

"I'm glad my misery could bring you such enjoyment."

He grabbed hold of her arm, and tried unsuccessfully to stop laughing at her. "Don't be mad, Danetta. Plenty of women have to provide their men with gas money and health insurance."

She snatched her arm out of his grasp. "Let me go call Veronica and tell her where you're at, so you can wave your little restraining order in her face."

He stopped laughing. Frowned. "That's a low blow, D. You know I didn't want to get a restraining order on that woman, but she is seriously off her meds."

They sat in silence for a while, both licking their dating wounds. Danetta's eyes began to droop. She leaned her head on Marshall's shoulder and drifted off to sleep. Marshall watched her sleeping form until his own weariness took over and he leaned his head against hers and closed his eyes.

Not long after, the doctor walked out and

woke them up. "Are you here for Sarah Davis?"

Stretching and rubbing her eyes, Danetta said, "Yes, I'm her niece."

"Well your aunt is resting now, but the tests we ran show that she had a heart attack and she has three blocked arteries. We're getting a room ready for her now."

"She has to stay . . . here?" Danetta asked in horror.

He gave her a look that seemed to ask, *are you stupid?* Then in his most professional-sounding voice he said, "There's no way that your aunt will be able to leave this hospital. We will most likely need to do surgery, but she isn't strong enough for that right now."

Tears filled her eyes. Marshall put his arm around her waist and pulled her close to him. "Can I see her?" Danetta asked.

"We just gave her a sedative so she can sleep. I'm hoping that she regains some of her strength with a little rest. So, it would be best for her if you could wait until tomorrow."

She turned to Marshall with fear in her eyes. "They're not going to let me see her."

"That's not what he said, Danetta. The doctor thinks it's best if you wait until tomorrow so she can get some rest."

"B-but I want to see her."

Rubbing her back he softly said, "How about we let her get some rest, D. We can come back first thing in the morning."

She hesitated, and then nodded.

Marshall turned to the doctor. "Thanks for giving us an update. We will check back with the hospital in case there are any changes."

"Yes, of course. She should have a room shortly and then you can contact the nurse station on her floor."

Danetta waited until her aunt had been assigned a room and then Marshall drove her home. As they pulled up in front of her house, she continued to sit in Marshall's car, looking at her house but making no attempt to go to it.

"Do you want me to come inside with you?" Marshall asked.

Danetta turned to him and admitted, "I don't want to be alone tonight."

They walked silently to her door, hand in hand.

CHAPTER 12

"Do you want something to drink?"

"Whatcha got?"

She opened the refrigerator and peeked in. "Iced tea, milk and bottled water."

He really wanted a nice stiff drink. After the day Danetta had, he thought she needed one too, but he knew she didn't drink, so he wasn't about to suggest it. "Iced tea, please."

She opened a pack of oatmeal cookies with white icing on top, spread them out on a plate, poured their drinks and then took the stuff to the living room. They sat down on the couch and after taking a sip of her tea, Danetta put her feet up on the couch and laid her head on Marshall's shoulder. This man meant so much to her. She had been in love with him a moment after meeting him in college. But he'd never felt the same way about her, so she had accepted his friendship and tried to let that be enough.

But lately, Marshall had been looking at her differently. She'd seen desire in his eyes several times in the last few weeks. He seemed to try to find reasons to be near her and to touch her. And why did he keep bringing up her dates, if he wasn't a little bit jealous? That's when Danetta remembered the 'husband list' she'd made years ago. Marshall stood head and shoulders above every man she knew when it came to meeting those requirements. He just didn't meet the top one . . . she wanted a man she could trust with her heart. But maybe that kind of trust grows with time, she reasoned.

And if the way he'd been acting lately was any indication, maybe Marshall was willing to give love a try — with her. But there was no way she could ask him. Her wound still hadn't healed from the time he turned her down in college. She adjusted her head and their eyes locked. He was looking at her that way again . . . as if she was all that mattered and the heat that blazed in his eyes was for her only. Not knowing what to say or do, she was the first to blink and look away.

He put his hand on her chin and turned her back to face him. "You're beautiful, you know that?"

She opened her mouth trying to find

something glib to say, but before she could get a word out, his mouth covered hers and she felt the heat of his passion as their lips and then tongues met. And just that quick, she didn't care that this man had turned her away in college or that she had spent a lifetime pining over him while he chased after other women. None of that mattered as she allowed herself to become lost in him.

He deepened the kiss as he lowered her down onto the couch. She took in the smell of him, ran her hands over his strong shoulders and back. She loved the way his muscles rippled and flexed as he explored her curves and planes. She had some major plans for this man tonight! She unlooped his tie and threw it across the room. His hands were everywhere at once, and then he began unbuttoning her blouse. Her pent-up passion had finally been unleashed and Danetta wanted to scream out loud. Marshall was working magic with his mouth and hands. She wanted to be closer to him, skin to skin with sweat dripping from their bodies as they made slow intoxicating love. "Oooh, Marshall," she cooed as he undid the last button and then planted his hands on her body again.

At the sound of Danetta's sweet voice, Marshall's hands stopped moving; he stared down at her. This was *his Danetta.* His friend and his confidant. He couldn't just take her to bed and then wake up in the morning and act as if nothing had happened, the way he'd been able to do with most of the women he'd dated through the years. Marshall knew deep in his soul that this act would change them forever. Was he ready for that? He sat up and pulled Danetta with him.

"W-what, what's wrong?"

"What are we doing, Danetta?"

"I thought we were doing some pretty good stuff," she said as she put her arms around his neck and tried to pull him back down.

He lightly kissed her lips, but removed her arms. "We need to talk about this, hon. You and I have been friends for a long time and I don't want to lose you."

Here he goes with that friend stuff again.

"What are you looking for, Danetta? If we make love tonight, do you want us to be in a relationship? Are you looking for a 'til-death-do-us-part kind of commitment?"

Yes and yes. She knew Marshall desired her right now, but that didn't mean he wanted a relationship. But she wanted this night, even if it meant that he would break her heart in the morning. So, she tried to look as cavalier as possible as she said, "You think I've never had sex just for the purpose of having sex before? Look, the truth is, I need this and I'd rather have sex with you, than one of the men I recently met." She shrugged her shoulders as she continued to lie. "But it's no big deal . . . no strings attached."

He jumped off the couch and started buttoning his shirt back up. He'd said the same thing to countless women in his past, but he'd never realized just how much those words stung. And as Danetta basically told him that all she needed was a warm body tonight, he realized that she wasn't that into him, anybody could be here and she still would have responded the same way.

Confused by the look of hurt on Marshall's face, Danetta asked, "What's wrong? Why are you buttoning your shirt?"

"I'm not about to let you use me as your boy toy," Marshall said angrily. "You can forget that."

"What's wrong with you? I thought we both wanted this. I was just letting you know that I'm not trying to tie you down. I just want to spend the night with you, Marshall." She pleaded with him. "I need you."

He searched around for his tie, found it

158

and then threw it around his neck. "Call up one of your other men and see if one of them will let you use their body."

She was so confused by his response that she couldn't say anything. She stood there with her blouse open and her Victoria's Secret bra exposed.

He pointed an accusing finger at her as he raged on. "You are the one person I would have never expected something like this from, Danetta. I don't even think I know you anymore."

Hot anger slid up her spine. She put her hands on her hips and strutted over to him. "I haven't changed. I'm the same person I've always been on the inside. But it's mighty funny that you didn't seem to notice me until I threw on a little more makeup and started wearing clothes that showed off my figure."

He opened his mouth to deny it, but she shut him down.

"If it's not true, then explain how come, in all the years I've known you, I've never seen lust in your eyes when you looked at me until the last few weeks? Huh?"

"I-I . . ."

"Cat got your tongue? Or you just can't think of a good enough lie to tell?"

"I have always cared about you, Danetta!"

he screamed at her.

She flailed her arms and screamed back at him, "You didn't care enough, though, did you?"

His eyes smoldered as he stared at her; he averted his eyes and said, "Button your shirt."

She looked down and noticed that more of her breasts were exposed than she realized. But instead of feeling embarrassed, she became emboldened. She took her shirt off and flung it onto the floor. She lifted her chest and taunted him. "What's the matter, Marshall? Am I too much woman for you? Is that why you've run around here with all those empty-headed beauties . . . because you can't handle a real woman?"

"I'm going to get out of here before we say and do something that will affect our ability to work together." He grabbed the door handle, jerked open the door and stormed out of the house.

The door slammed behind Marshall as Danetta continued to defiantly stand in the middle of her living room in nothing but her skirt and bra. Tears stung her eyes as humiliation swept over her. She'd thrown herself at Marshall once again, and he'd rejected her, as if what she was offering was worth nothing.

Her phone rang. She wanted to ignore it, but Aunt Sarah was in the hospital and she couldn't miss a call from the hospital, no matter how much she felt like hiding under a rock. She glanced at the caller ID and saw that it was Ryla. Wiping the tears from her face, she picked up the phone. "Hello."

"Hey girl, I've been trying to reach you all day. Monica told me that your aunt is in the hospital."

Danetta flung herself onto the couch and began crying.

"Oh no, Danetta. I'm so sorry. I didn't even know that your aunt was ill."

From Ryla's response, Danetta figured that her friend thought that Aunt Sarah was dead, so she quickly said, "S-she had a heart attack. She's weak right now, but still alive."

"Girl, you were crying so hard, I thought she had passed away. I'm so glad that she's doing okay. But, what's going on with you?"

"Oh nothing," she said sarcastically. "Marshall just humiliated me again."

"What? How?"

Danetta told Ryla everything that had happened from the hospital visit until he stormed out of her door.

When she finished, Ryla asked, "Girl, you actually told that man that he was just a booty call?"

"I didn't use those words."

"He's sitting there asking if you want a relationship or marriage . . . men don't ask those questions for nothing."

"I thought he wanted me to say that stuff," Danetta explained. "Men love it when they can have sex with no strings attached."

Ryla was silent for a moment. "But maybe Marshall was hoping for something more and when he realized that you didn't feel the same way, his feelings got hurt."

"Are we talking about the same man? Marshall just had to get a restraining order on a woman because she was tired of his 'love-'em-and-leave-'em' hound dog behavior."

"Yeah, but Danetta, all I'm saying is that I've seen you and Marshall together throughout the years. I've always thought that he cares very deeply for you. Maybe he's finally realized that you are the woman for him."

Danetta shook her head. "And I say he's mad at himself because he now feels attracted to me, but he still wants to keep me in the friend zone. You know what . . . I don't care anymore, Ryla. I'm tired of caring. Matter-of-fact, I'm tired of this whole thing."

162

"What whole thing?"

"My Get Love Now plan has backfired in my face. Every last man I've gone out with so far has been a loser and I don't want to do this anymore. Please delete my profile from those dating websites that you posted my information on."

"But, Danetta, how do you think you're going to meet the right man if you don't go through a few duds first?"

"I never should have let you talk me into something like this. Going out with these random men is just not my style. And I really need to get Marshall out of my head before I can think about dating another man."

"Like my grandmother says, 'the best way to get over one man is to get under another one.' "

Danetta gasped. "Your granny said that?"

"Let me tell you," Ryla laughed, "My grandmother is a hot mess. I have seen and heard things from that woman that made me want to puncture my eardrums and pull my eyeballs out of my head. But I think she's right on this issue."

"I can't do that, Ryla. Just cancel my memberships on those sites. I'm going to bed. I'll talk to you tomorrow."

Misery was etched across Marshall's face as he walked into Kevin's house and said, "She wanted to have her way with me, no strings attached."

"You say that like it's a bad thing," Kevin said while popping Marshall in the back of the head. "Are you telling me that you passed up some free love? Dawg, you slippin'?"

"She played me, man."

"She tried to hook up with you, but you were too busy looking a gift horse in the mouth to appreciate the beauty in her statement." He shook his head in disgust. "Playa, playa, what has happened to you?"

"Are you listening to me, Kevin? I asked the woman if she wanted a relationship or marriage and she told me that sex between us would be no big deal." He stood up and paced the room. He was truly stumped by Danetta's cavalier attitude toward sex. He turned back to Kevin as he remembered another part of the conversation. "And then she had the nerve to say that she'd rather have sex with me than any of the men she'd been out with lately. Like, if I said no, she would just go call one of them."

Now Kevin had to sit down. "You actually mentioned marriage to her?"

"Like a fool," Marshall said. His face contorted as he ran his hands over his face and head. "I really care about Danetta, and I thought she felt the same way about me. But she's changed."

Kevin got up, went to his closet and pulled out a jacket. He grabbed his car keys and said, "Come on."

"What? Where are we going?"

"Look, you're my boy. And believe it or not, I do understand this little midlife crisis thing you're going through. But you need to snap out of it. I'm taking you to the club tonight so you can get yo' drink on and find a woman that will get Danetta off your mind."

"Sleeping with some woman tonight is not going stop me from thinking about Danetta, because I see the woman every day. We work together, in case you forgot."

"You're not working with her right now, are you?"

"Of course not, I'm over here."

"That's right," Kevin said with a sly smile. "And I'm going to take you out so you can snuggle up with some hottie and get your mind back right."

Marshall shook his head as he laughed.

165

Maybe Kevin was right, maybe he needed to find a warm body and get his mack on. Danetta didn't want him, but one thing Marshall knew for sure . . . the ladies loved him.

CHAPTER 13

Marshall and Kevin stood in the VIP area bobbing their heads to the beat of a Jay-Z song. The drinks were flowing, the music was bumping, the women were fine and the dance floor was packed, but as Marshall glanced around the room, he found himself wondering if everyone there was as bored as he.

As the music changed to a slow song, a woman dressed in a Gucci pantsuit with handbag and eyeglasses to match stepped to Marshall with a flirty look in her eyes. "Hey, Marshall, what's up?"

"Not much, Shelly. What's been up with you?"

"Oh a little of this and a little of that," she countered as she ran her hands through her long silky black hair.

"Is that right?" he said while looking around the room. A yawn escaped his lips and he didn't even bother to cover it. Glancing at his watch, he wanted nothing more than to go home and get some sleep.

"Did you hear me?" Shelly asked as she nudged Marshall's shoulder.

"Huh, what?"

"I asked if you wanted to dance. They're playing my slow jam, and if you play your cards right, this could become our song." She flirted with every word that left her mouth.

Shelly was fine and had a lightweight modeling career going on. A while back he had thought about asking her out, but now he couldn't even muster up enough interest to get on the dance floor with her. "I'm a little tired, but maybe later, all right?"

She shrugged. As she walked away from him she said, "Your loss."

Yeah, my loss, Marshall thought as he sat down in a chair in the back of the VIP section. This was one of the more popular clubs in town for professionals. The place was packed. Men with degrees and good-paying jobs were in the house, so the women naturally followed. Marshall had spent many nights in this place — dancing, drinking and hooking up with one woman after the next. As he thought about that fact, he felt kind of hypocritical for being so upset about Danetta's attitude toward them hooking up. Hadn't he told countless women that he wanted sex with no strings? But right now Marshall was thinking that there had to be more out of life, and he was determined to find it.

"Man, what are you doing hiding in this dark corner?" Kevin asked as he approached Marshall. He stretched out a hand and waved toward the dance floor. "Will you look at them, man? It's like Christmas came early," Kevin said while letting his eyes do the walking up a long-legged female's thigh.

Marshall was in a foul mood. He didn't want to be there, so he had no problem raining on someone else's good time. "Kevin, why are you up here frontin' like you gon' step to that woman? When I know and you know that Marla's got you on lock."

"Who me?" Kevin took a step back. "Uh-uh. Not me, not happening."

"You know what bothers me about you, Kevin?" Marshall poked a finger in his friend's chest. "You've got a good woman who loves you, but instead of doing right by her, you'd rather do something dumb and mess it all up."

"Well, hello pot," Kevin said with a smirk of irritation on his face.

"I am nothing like you, bro. If I had a woman who loved me like your girl, I wouldn't be out here trying to get into something that won't even matter in the morning."

Irritation turned to anger and Kevin spat, "You had somebody and you did her worse than I've ever done Marla, believe that."

Marshall waved him off. "You don't know what you're talking about."

"Oh, so you think it was just fine to parade all those women in Danetta's face year after year while she sat there taking care of your business and probably crying herself to sleep every night?"

"Danetta and I are just friends. And weren't you listening to me earlier? I told you she wanted no strings attached. Does that sound like somebody in love?"

"Payback is a mother, ain't it?" A waitress walked up to him with the drink he had ordered. Kevin took it from her, downed it in one swallow and then turned back to Marshall. "Look, man, you obviously don't want to be here. So, why don't you just go home."

"I rode here with you, remember?"

"That's right, so sit down somewhere and shut up."

He knew that if he opened his mouth at that moment he would lose a friend. So he turned and stalked off.

"Hey, come on, bro, don't leave mad," Kevin called after him.

Marshall threw up a hand. "I'm out." He pushed and shoved his way through the crowd.

When he stepped outside Marshall asked the valet to call a cab for him. Feeling like a chump who'd lost in the game of life, he stood with shoulders slumped, waiting for the cab. The door to the club kept swinging open as groups of people left and more party-goers arrived. They had the look of expectation on their young pretty faces, as if they hadn't blown through that door a hundred times and received the same good-for-nothing results. He didn't know why people didn't tire of places like this . . . that could only offer twenty-four-hour relationships that left you waiting by the phone for the call that never comes. Then the eventual shame begins to creep in for what a woman would do in the wee hours of the morning for a man who wouldn't even remember her name the next day. But they come back to the club the very next week, dressed in their best, and ready to commit insanity once again.

As he continued to watch women walk into the club and men creep out of the club with arms draped around some unsuspecting woman, anger penetrated his soul. It was at that moment that he decided that he no longer wanted to be a part of that game. He wondered if he would be absolved of all his wrongdoing if he gave these women the 411 right now. Or maybe he needed to go find a priest . . . sit in that booth and tell the man about all the women he had tricked. Maybe if he remembered all of his misdeeds, he wouldn't feel so bad about the way Danetta had treated him like a piece of meat tonight.

He still didn't understand why he was so angry with her. Why hadn't he stayed and taken what she was freely offering to him? Hadn't she said that she'd rather be with him than any of the other men she'd been dating? But who would she want to be with next week, or next month?

His head was starting to hurt with all of this thinking. He put his hand to his temple to rub it. And that's when he saw her. He still didn't remember the woman's name, but this time he had no problem recognizing her on sight. He rarely forgot the faces of women who slapped him. The last time he saw this beautiful woman had been at the business retreat he'd attended about a month ago. She'd been angry with him because he'd slept with her and then never called. At the time, he couldn't understand her anger and had even told her that she knew what time it was when she stepped into his hotel room. But now he was beginning to see the light.

Her purse was swinging and she had keys in hand as she stepped out of the club. He tapped her on the shoulder. "Excuse me."

She turned, smiling, toward him. Once she recognized who was standing in front of her, the smile got lost in a sea of frowns. "What do you want?"

"I — I, uh."

"Spit it out, I don't have all night."

Just give me a moment, Ms., 'I can spend all night with you in bed, but I can't spend ten seconds waiting on you to come up with a coherent thought.' That's what he wanted to say, but he had the good grace to say, "I just wanted to apologize to you."

Hands on hips, she put the sistah-sistah neck roll in action. "Look, I don't know if you are drunk or what, but I suggest you get out of my face. I'm the kinda sistah who carries mace and I will use it on a dog like you."

He held up his hands fending her off. "You wanted me to get mine, so that I would know how you felt . . . remember? Well, it happened. And you were right, I didn't like the way it felt to know that someone only wanted me for one thing." He shrugged. "So, I'm sorry for the way I treated you, okay?"

As her hands came down off her hips, her guard also seemed to fall. "I'll tell you what . . . say my name and I'll forgive you."

Marshall's face dropped. He would have been better off in that confessional booth. So many one-night stands with nameless, faceless women who all thought they were putting it on him so tough that he'd never be able to forget them, but in truth, the women had all melded into one. In the midnight hour, he'd found nothing different, nothing special about the sex that any one of the women had given him to make him want to stay. Maybe he was finally growing up, because he'd never felt bad about any of this stuff before.

"That's why I'm apologizing," he began. "When I had sex with you I wasn't thinking about who you were as a person, what puts a smile on your face or anything like that."

"So, you're admitting that you don't know my name?"

Shame crossed his face as he nodded. "But I'd like to know now."

She cocked her head to the side and grinned at him. "What do you want to know . . . who I am as a person or what puts a smile on my face?"

"Let's just start with your name."

"All right, it's Marrisa Miller."

The cab pulled up. Marshall stuck out his hand. "Nice to meet you, Marrisa." As they shook hands, Marshall wondered if he would have been able to develop a relationship with this woman if he had given it half a chance. He probably would never know. "This is my cab, but it was nice seeing you again, Marrisa." He turned and began walking toward the cab.

Marrisa yelled, "Wait . . . don't you want to know the rest?"

Marshall turned back to face her. "Why don't you give me your number and I'll take you out to lunch so we can talk. I promise I'll do nothing but listen."

She shook her head and lifted her keys for him to see. "You're not getting away that easy. Send your cab away and I'll drive you home."

He looked at her skeptically for a moment and then asked, "You just want to talk, right? Because I don't need any more guilt on my shoulders about being a 'love 'em and leave 'em' kind of guy." Marshall couldn't believe his own ears. Was he actually turning down sex for the second time in one night? Forget the priest, maybe he needed to see a shrink instead.

She dangled the keys again. "I've got a lot I'd like to tell you. And I'd like to have your undivided attention while I've got it."

"Okay then, I'm down with that." He waved the cab off and headed toward the parking lot with Marrisa Miller. He didn't know anything about this woman, except her name, but he had a feeling that before the night was over he would discover everything that made Marrisa tick, and none of his discoveries would be made between the sheets. The knowledge of that actually put a smile on his face.

Danetta had a fitful night's sleep. She kept seeing Marshall's horrorstruck face as she told him that she just needed sex from him, and nothing more. But she'd thought that he'd wanted to hear that. He had bragged to her and his friend Kevin dozens of times about the countless women to whom he'd said the same thing. So, she didn't understand his reaction at all.

As bad as that had been, the way they spoke to each other had been worse. She'd never talked to Marshall like that before and he'd never so much as raised his voice at her. She didn't know where the partnership stood, but one thing was clear to Danetta: their friendship had suffered a blow. After talking to Ryla, the anger Danetta had felt toward Marshall had subsided, because she realized that Ryla might have been right and she might have read Marshall's intentions all wrong.

At about five in the morning, Danetta got out of bed and went for a run. She hadn't done that in months, but she needed to clear out the cobwebs, and she wasn't getting any sleep anyway. When she arrived back at the house, she jumped in the shower and then changed into a jogging suit. She wasn't going into work that day; there was no way she would be able to concentrate with everything that was going on with her aunt and with Marshall. Danetta had made up her mind to drive to Marshall's house that morning and clear the air. Then she would go to the hospital and sit with her aunt.

She opened her top dresser drawer where she kept a few of her accessories and pulled out a pair of dark shades. There was no sun in the sky that day, but Danetta didn't need the glasses to protect her from the sun. Her game plan to get to her aunt's hospital bed without experiencing another anxiety attack was to enter the hospital through a door that she had never walked through before and to wear her shades, so that she could see as little of those dreaded corridors and hospital rooms as possible.

She got in her car and drove to Marshall's house. She had to talk to him, because there was no way they would be able to work together without coming to an understanding about what happened between them the night before. But as she sat in her car in front of his house, Danetta didn't know what to do. A car was in his driveway that Danetta had never seen before.

She had convinced herself to drive away and just call Marshall on the phone so that they could talk about their problems, when the front door opened. A laughing woman with sparkling eyes and a long flowing weave stepped out of Marshall's house. Marshall walked out behind her and closed his door. He put his arm around the woman as they walked to his driveway; they were both laughing and smiling as if they were about to bust a gut over something one of them had said. As Danetta eyed them, she wondered if maybe Marshall was telling a joke about his dumber-than-a-box-of-rocks business partner, who'd foolishly offered him her body, but he hadn't wanted it. And why would he want plain ol' Danetta Harris when he could be with someone as beautiful as the woman he was now laughing it up with?

They stopped at the woman's car. Marshall kissed her on the forehead; she smiled, touched his cheek and then got into her car and drove off. Marshall got in his SUV and started backing out of the driveway. It was then, as he turned his head to look for oncoming traffic that his eyes locked with Danetta's. If looks could kill he would have, at the very least, been hospitalized and told that he'd barely escaped with his life.

Marshall put his car in Park, got out and began walking toward Danetta's car. Danetta sped off.

Tears streamed down her face as she broke speed limits in order to get away from Marshall. How could he do this to her? How could he make her feel bad about wanting to spend the night with him, when he clearly wasn't above one-night stands. Why did he try to act so offended when he could have just told her the truth? That it wasn't the one-night stand that bothered him — he just didn't want to be with her.

Fearing that she was looking like a maniac to some of the drivers on the street, she wiped the tears from her face. But when another river flow replaced the last one, she banged her hand on the steering wheel and screamed. Life was just not, not, not fair.

She stopped at a red light and again tried to fix her appearance. But as she wiped away the tears this time, Danetta noticed a donut shop that was calling her name. She pulled into the parking lot and got out of her car.

Inside the donut shop, which was really no more than a hole-in-the-wall type of place, there were so few customers that they actually had a mannequin in one of the window seats. Danetta didn't care, she just needed a sugar fix and she needed it now.

"How you doing, honey?" the cashier asked with a bit of a southern drawl.

"Not too good," Danetta answered. "But I think three brownies and two wheat donuts will get me through it."

CHAPTER 14

She made it to her aunt's room without breaking down and having herself strapped to a gurney and wheeled to the fifth floor where they had the nice padded rooms. Her plan was to take her sunglasses off once she sat down with Aunt Sarah, but since she'd been crying her eyes out and they were now red and swollen, she thought it best to leave them on.

"How are you feeling today, Aunt Sarah?"

Her aunt had several pillows behind her head, propping her up in the bed. She turned to Danetta and said, "Oh I'm fair to middlin'. But I'm more concerned about you and why you have sunglasses on when it looks quite cloudy out my window."

"To tell you the truth, Auntie . . ." *well, she could tell part of the truth anyway,* "I had a panic attack when I walked through the emergency room yesterday. If Marshall hadn't been with me, I probably would have ended up in the bed next to yours. So, I decided to wear these glasses to block out some of my vision as I walked to your room."

"I'm glad you were able to break through your fears, sweetie." She patted Danetta's hands. "And I'm sorry that the ambulance brought me to this hospital. This is the last thing I ever wanted to do to you."

"I know that. It's not your fault."

"Okay, well then take those shades off and watch some TV with me."

Danetta hesitated, but she knew there was no way around it. Her aunt would not rest until she took the glasses off. To keep the peace — her aunt was, after all, a heart patient — she did as she was told. The glasses came off and Danetta grabbed the remote so that she could find a program for them to watch together. "What do you want to see this morning?"

Aunt Sarah didn't answer. She was too busy studying Danetta. She lifted Danetta's chin and turned her face toward her.

Danetta averted her eyes. "Oh, they have the Hallmark Channel. You love watching the movies on that channel."

"What's wrong, baby? Tell me what happened."

"If you don't want to watch the Hallmark

Channel, they also have the Turner Classic Network and TBN, the station that all those preachers come on."

Aunt Sarah took the remote out of Danetta's hand. "Talk to me; I can tell that something is wrong. And I have a feeling that it has nothing to do with me laying in this hospital bed."

She had never been able to hide anything from her aunt. Sometimes, Danetta thought that her aunt knew her better than she knew herself. She put the remote down. "I'm so embarrassed, Auntie, I don't even know where to begin."

"Did something happen with one of them men you've been dating?"

She shook her head.

"Well then it has to be Marshall. What did he do that's got you so upset?"

Anger flared in Danetta's nostrils as she said, "He didn't do anything. That was the problem. I all but threw myself at him last night and h-he turned me down."

"What do you mean, he turned you down? What did he say?"

Danetta really hated talking about these things with her aunt. She knew how Sarah Davis felt about promiscuity. It had been drilled into her head so much, that Danetta had rarely gone all the way with a guy. "He asked me if I was looking for a relationship or for marriage and I told him no, that he didn't have to worry about that. We could just, you know —" she had the good sense to be embarrassed by what she was about to say, "— hook up, no strings attached. And then he got mad and accused me of just trying to use him for sex. I couldn't believe the way he reacted about the whole thing."

"Well, dear, the man clearly wants more from you than just a hook-up, as you young people say. And I certainly can't be mad at him for that."

Danetta wanted to tell her aunt how she knew that that wasn't true. Marshall didn't mind hooking up with women. He just didn't want any part of *her*. But that would have been more humiliation than she could stand.

"I have always thought that you and Marshall would make a wonderful couple," Sarah beamed.

"It's not going to happen, so you can get that out of your head. Marshall clearly wants nothing to do with me."

"I think you're seeing this all wrong. Why don't you pray for God to reveal Marshall's true feelings for you?"

Danetta balked. "Are you joking?"

Sarah leaned back against her pillows. "No, I'm not. If Marshall doesn't know what's good for him by now, God can surely reveal it to him."

"Well I'm not about to pray to God for no man or anything else for that matter. I have taken care of myself for a long time now and I will take care of this problem without the help of some so-called supreme power, thank you very much."

The room went silent. Nothing but the beep of the monitors could be heard for a long while. After a moment, Sarah broke the silence. "In the book of Daniel, there are three Hebrew boys, Shadrach, Meshach and Abednego. These three Hebrew boys loved God kinda the way you used to love Him before your mama went home. Anyway, Shadrach, Meshach and Abednego wouldn't bow down to the king nor would they worship the golden images the king thought were some kind of gods.

"So, one day the king threatened to have them thrown into a fiery furnace unless they bowed down to him and his gods. The king told them that their God wouldn't be able to rescue them from such a thing."

"I think I've heard this story before."

Aunt Sarah ignored her. "But those three Hebrew boys didn't pay the king no mind.

185

They told him that even if their God didn't rescue them from the furnace, they still believed that He was able and that was good enough for them."

"So what's your point, Auntie?"

"My point is, you've lost your even-if-I-don't-see-it-come-to-pass-I-still-believe-He's-able kind of faith that causes God to move on your behalf."

What could she say? Her aunt was right. She hadn't thought about God, the Bible or church for so long now that there was no way she could claim to have faith in anything but herself anymore. And truth be told, Danetta didn't much care. She didn't need some invisible God in the sky.

"After I saw how much it bothered you to come into this hospital last night, I prayed and prayed, asking God why the hospital that was closest to my home had been filled to capacity, and therefore I had to be brought here. And after much prayer, I figured out why I'm here."

"You have three clogged arteries, that's why you're here," Danetta told her, not wanting to listen to any more.

"I know my arteries are clogged. I'm talking about the reason I'm at this particular hospital. It's for you, Danetta."

"For me!" Danetta exploded at the ludicrous statement. "Exactly how much pain medicine do they have you on, Auntie?"

"Not enough, however much it is. Now be quiet and let me tell you what I know." She looked at Danetta with sorrowful eyes, as she said, "God showed me that you didn't just lose your mother in this hospital . . . you lost your faith here also. And He's going to use me and my situation to bring it back."

If anything, her aunt's situation was making her angry at God all over again. Here He was, trying to take somebody else away from her, and her aunt thought that she was suddenly going to bow down and thank Him for this. The nurse came in to take her aunt's temperature and blood pressure, saving her from having to respond to all the nonsense she'd just heard. She wanted to tell the nurse to ease up on the pain medication, but didn't want to cause her aunt more pain, just to stop all the crazy talk.

Danetta ate her brownies for breakfast. When it was time for lunch, she put her shades on to walk to the cafeteria, but Aunt Sarah asked if she would try to walk to the cafeteria without her shades. Danetta tried and succeeded. She ate her wheat donuts after lunch, so by three in the afternoon, she was in need of another sugar fix.

Danetta left the hospital and stopped at the donut shop around the corner from her house. She was thankful that it was Friday so she didn't have to worry about going to work and facing Marshall the next day.

Marshall knew he was in trouble the moment he saw the devastated look on Danetta's face. He'd gotten out of his car and began walking to her car so that they could talk. He knew that she was thinking he had slept with Marissa, when nothing could be further from the truth. He and Marissa had such a good conversation on the way to pick up his car from Kevin's house that he invited her to follow him home. He'd fixed burgers and fries for them and they'd continued talking.

At no time during the night had he made a move to sleep with Marissa, nor had she tried anything with him. But something magical had happened last night; he and Marissa had become friends. She'd actually offered him and Danetta the chance to bid on an advertising project with her company. During the night he'd confessed to Marissa, and himself, that he felt as if he was falling in love with his business partner — why else would he have been so upset about the fact that she wasn't interested in a commitment from him?

Marissa had suggested that he tell Danetta how he felt, and Marshall had planned to do just that, but she drove like the devil himself was after her as he walked down his driveway toward her car. Marshall got in his car and drove to work, thinking that he would be able to talk to Danetta there, but just as he was about to knock on Danetta's office door, Monica came back to her desk, cup of coffee in hand.

"She's not in."

"Is she running late?" Marshall asked casually.

"No. She's going to spend the day with her aunt at the hospital."

"Oh, okay," Marshall said as he walked away. He didn't want to call Aunt Sarah's room and disturb her while she was trying to rest, so he called Danetta's cell. It went straight to her voice mail. He called her cell ten times within a two-hour time span, but it continued to go straight to her voice mail. Marshall had left a few messages, but decided to stop after message number three.

By the time he put his phone down and decided to concentrate on work, his secretary buzzed him. "What's up, Stephanie?" he asked as he answered the intercom on his desk.

"You have a visitor at the front desk."

"Who is it?"

Sheepishly, Stephanie said, "The guard said it's Veronica."

"Oh my lawd." Marshall stood up. He rubbed his temples as he tried to decide what to do . . . call the police or confront his stalker. He was a man. He wasn't going to just let some boo-boo the fool punk him out like this. Veronica might know how to act crazy . . . slashing tires and keying cars, but he had a few tricks of his own. He opened his office door and headed for the elevator like a man with a plan.

When he made it to the lobby and Veronica was standing next to the guard's desk holding up a picnic basket and a big smile, he halted his stride. *Just how crazy was this woman?*

"Happy Friday," she said in a singsong voice.

Veronica used to bring him lunch on Fridays when they were dating. He'd greedily eaten every morsel of the food at that time, but now that he knew what he did about this woman, he'd sooner eat cat food than anything in that basket. "You do know that I have a restraining order against you, right?"

"You still have to eat." Her words were

190

still sing-songy.

Whether he would admit it or not, Marshall's knees were knocking together. At that moment he was thankful that he didn't have a pet. Veronica probably would have boiled it up and then tried to serve his own pet to him for lunch. "I'm not hungry. And you need to get out of here before I call the police."

"Why so hostile, baby? Tell mama whatsamatter, so I can make it all better."

Marshall made eye contact with the guard and said, "Call 911."

The flashlight cop actually looked offended that Marshall hadn't asked him to handle the situation. As he flexed his steroid biceps, he said, "I can take care of this, Mr. Windham."

Marshall spoke to the guard as if Veronica wasn't standing right there holding up her picnic basket and smiling like she was in a Colgate commercial. "Look, Ronnie, I'm sure you're very capable, but we're dealing with a real live nutty-buddy right here. I need an officer with a gun and some handcuffs."

"Stop playing, Marshall. I'm sorry about slashing your tires."

"And keying my car?"

"Yeah, that, too," she said as if she'd just

admitted to sneaking an extra cookie.

"I see what you mean," Ronnie said as he and his biceps went back behind the desk and picked up the phone.

Veronica's face dropped as she lowered the picnic basket. "Are you really going to let him call the police on me, baby?"

"I'm not your baby. Don't you get it? We are over. And if we hadn't been over before, all this stalking you've been doing has surely made me think twice about ever getting involved with you again."

Tears streamed down Veronica's face. "But we were good together."

Marshall shook his head. "Not that good." Veronica had been a poor man's substitute for Danetta. Like ordering chicken when you were hungry enough to eat steak and lobster, but couldn't afford what your taste buds were screaming for. When Danetta had come to him back in college wanting to hook up, Marshall had known then that being with a woman like Danetta would cost him much more than he could afford to pay at that time. So, he'd spent a lifetime settling for less than what his heart really wanted.

"B-but, but —"

He held up a hand. "Look Veronica, I'm not trying to hurt you, but you really need to understand something. It is simply this . . . I will never take you back. It really has nothing to do with what you did to my car. The truth is, I just don't want to be with you. And nothing you do is going to make me want you back. Do you understand?"

As if a miracle was unfolding right before his eyes, Veronica's eyes lit with understanding. She set the picnic basket on the guard's desk and began walking to the door. She said, "I won't bother you again." Without looking back at him, she walked out of the door and out of his life.

Marshall and Ronnie both let out a sigh.

"Man, I thought she was going to pick up the letter opener on my desk and gut you. I wouldn't have ever been that honest with a psycho crazy woman like that." Ronnie said, while fist bumping Marshall, "You're my new hero."

Marshall didn't want to be anybody's hero. He just wanted to be left alone. Well, that wasn't exactly true. There was one woman in his life that he wanted to be bothered with every day from here until eternity. He made up his mind, right then and there, that he was going to clear up a few things on his desk and then go to Danetta's house and sit and wait on her like a stalker. He just hoped that she loved him enough to listen to what he had to say.

CHAPTER 15

Danetta's mouth was watering as she stood in line getting ready to order a half dozen brownies covered with chocolate icing and macadamia nuts sprinkled on top, when someone tapped her on the shoulder. She turned and found Stan the flex-hour man. He was wearing a suit and tie, holding on to a binder in one hand and a donut box in the other. Stan was looking so good to her, standing there in business attire, like a man with a plan rather than a man in need of health insurance that she forgot all about those chocolate goodies behind the donut counter and her mouth started watering for him. "Stan, what are you doing on this side of town?" she asked as she stepped out of line.

"I had a meeting with a client. He lives on Nina Lee Lane, so he wanted to meet here."

"You're kidding, I live on Nina Lee Lane," Danetta said and then clamped her mouth shut. She couldn't believe that she'd just told a guy she barely knew which street she lived on.

"Hey, how's your aunt doing?" Stan asked as he guided her over to an empty table.

They sat down. "She needs surgery. It's her heart."

"That's too bad." He shook his head at the sad news. "How are you holding up?"

Stan was acting as if her issues mattered to him, and she liked that. Maybe she misjudged him during their first date. "To tell you the truth, I'm not doing so good. Having to see my aunt in that hospital bed is one of the hardest things I've had to do in a long while."

"Sounds like you need a sugar fix." He lifted the box he'd been holding. "I have brownies and donuts."

Flirting a bit with her eyes, Danetta slung her hair back and asked, "Are you trying to get another date out of me?"

He leaned in closer. "I'd love another date with you, especially since I'm celebrating."

"What are you celebrating?"

"My client just signed off on the contract for a serious remodel to his house. So, the work will keep me busy for the next month." Stan smiled at his good fortune, and his dimples did a little dance.

This pretty boy had it going on. Dimples and a job . . . what else could she ask for? Although a date with Stan was sounding real good right about now, she just wasn't up for it. "I'm exhausted right now and just want to go home and rest." She stood up. "Why don't you give me a call next week and we can go out to dinner or something."

"Or," he said with those deep dimples showing again, "you could invite me over . . . offer me some coffee or tea and I'll share my treats with you." He shook the box in her face trying to entice her to seeing things his way

His eyes told her that he was interested in more than health insurance today, and he suddenly looked quite irresistible. She threw caution to the wind, pointed to her car just outside the donut shop and said, "I have tea. Follow me home and make sure you bring those brownies with you."

"Well then, let's get going." He opened the door and held it as Danetta walked out of the donut shop.

As Danetta pulled out of the parking lot, she began having second thoughts. Did she really want to hook up with Stan? She didn't know much about Stan, and even though he acted as if he had sense today, she hadn't been all that impressed with their first meeting. But then she thought about how Marshall rejected her. The sting of that rejection propelled her forward. She drove home with Stan following behind.

Marshall rarely left work early. He believed in playing hard, but working harder. However, the day had been a bust for him. He just hadn't been able to get the look on Danetta's face out of his mind. She appeared so wounded this morning after seeing him with Marissa. The worst part about the entire scene was that Danetta had it all wrong this time. He hadn't been running around sowing his oats. He'd been making amends for the wrong he'd done to a really nice woman who, under other circumstances, he might be inclined to start up a relationship with.

Right now all he wanted to do was clear the air with Danetta and help her to understand that he was not the same man who had turned her down in college. He had very different motives for what he said last night; Marshall just hoped that Danetta was in a listening mood. Shoot, who was he fooling, he really hoped that she was in the same mood she was in last night before he lost his mind and made a mess of everything.

He pulled up in front of Danetta's house

and turned off his car. Marshall was prepared to wait a lifetime on Danetta if need be.

As Danetta pulled into her driveway, she noticed Marshall parked in front of her house. She saw the smile on his face as he got out of his SUV and began walking toward her. Then Stan pulled into the driveway behind her and the smile left Marshall's face.

He opened her car door and demanded, "What's this dude doing here?"

Defiantly, she said, "I invited him over. Why? Where's the woman you were with this morning?"

Reflexes curled Marshall's fist as Stan got out of the car and headed toward Danetta. "What's this supposed to be, some sort of revenge against what you think I did?"

"Is everything all right, Danetta?" Stan asked as he approached.

Marshall turned on him. "No, everything is not all right."

"Ignore him, Stan. Come on, let's go in the house so we can get *comfy.*" Danetta made the word comfy sound X-rated as she grabbed Stan's arm and walked him to the front door.

Marshall buffed up and walked with them

into the house. "Oh, well then we all must be about to get comfy in here. Because we are not about to play this game, D."

Danetta was still holding on to the doorknob as she tried to usher Marshall back out of the house. "Go home, Marshall. What I do with my personal life does not concern you."

Marshall harrumphed. "You've lost your mind if you believe that." He pointed from Danetta to Stan and said, "This is not about to go down. Not before you hear me out."

"I don't have anything to say to you, Marshall. Now please leave. I have company."

Stan lifted a hand as he began walking back toward the front door. "Look, obviously you two have some drama going on that needs to be resolved." He stepped out of the door that Danetta had been holding open for Marshall. "Danetta, give me a call after you resolve . . ." he waved a finger between Danetta and Marshall, "whatever you've got going on here."

She slammed her front door as Stan got into his car and then turned back to Marshall. "Are you happy now? He'll probably never call me again."

"If that's the case, then I'm ecstatic." Marshall turned, looked out of the window and watched Stan back out of the driveway. He then turned back to Danetta and said, "Wasn't that the guy who wanted health insurance from you?"

"He wasn't looking for health insurance a few minutes ago." She poked a finger at her chest. "He just wanted me, and you ruined my chances with him."

"I don't believe this. You were actually thinking about getting with that guy?" When she didn't respond, Marshall said, "So, if I hadn't come over here, you would have slept with him, wouldn't you? Do you really need sex that bad?"

Now she was offended. With hands on hips she said, "Don't act stupid, Marshall. I don't have to sleep with every man who walks through my doors."

Lifting frustrated hands in the air, Marshall shouted, "What do you think he came over here for?"

"It's up to me to say yes or no."

"It's not so easy to tell a man no once you've already said yes, Danetta. Not too many men will let a woman get them all riled up and then let them change their minds."

Her irritation was rising. "You mean like how you did me last night? But funny thing is, I let you go without throwing you to the ground and going for mine anyway."

"You're twisting things around, because these are two totally different circumstances. You were trying to just hit it and quit it with me last night, and I don't want that between us."

She crossed her arms across her chest. "Oh, but it was okay for you to hit it and quit it with the woman who was at your house this morning."

The phone rang before he could respond to that. If her aunt wasn't in the hospital she would just let the phone ring and continue to watch Marshall squirm, but she couldn't do that. She turned her back to him and picked up the phone. "Hello. Yes, this is Danetta Harris."

After a moment of listening, Danetta gripped the table as tears sprang to her eyes.

"What's wrong?" Marshall asked, coming up behind her.

"Okay, okay." She was in full cry mode now. "I'll be right there."

"What happened?" Marshall tried again.

She hung up the phone and turned to face him. "My aunt just had another heart attack. They're taking her to surgery right now."

"I'll drive you to the hospital." He wiped some of the tears from her face, but the waterfall kept coming. "I don't want you trying to drive like this."

CHAPTER 16

As Marshall drove them to the hospital, an Otis Redding song came on the old-school radio station he listened to. Marshall started singing, "I've been lovin' you too long . . . can't stop now."

The song reminded her of the day that she and Marshall slow danced at their Valentine's party and right now, she desperately needed to forget. "Do you mind if I change this station?"

Marshall glanced over at Danetta. He wanted to object. He knew why she no longer had any tolerance for this song. But the reason she didn't want to hear it anymore was the reason he wanted to hear it over and over again . . . memories of their slow dance. But when he saw how tight her jaw was set, he said, "Go ahead."

Instead of changing the station, she pushed in the CD that Marshall had ejected out of the player the moment they got in the car. "When a Man Loves a Woman" boomed through the speakers. Marshall ejected the CD again and then switched the station to a radio talk show.

"Didn't want to waste your 'get in the mood' music on me, huh?" Danetta turned toward the window and began watching the white-and-yellow lines in the street.

"It's not like that, Danetta. You've got it all wrong."

She put a hand up and continued looking out the window.

She didn't believe him, and right now was not the time to plead his case. He kept driving down the street as he pushed the CD back in the player and allowed his heart to bleed over every lyric that Michael Bolton belted out, for Marshall truly would trade the world for just one more chance at Danetta's heart.

He pulled up at the front entrance of the hospital. Danetta jumped out of the car without looking back. She ran into the hospital and he sat there watching, making sure that she didn't go into another panic attack. Michael Bolton was still singing, reminding Marshall of the good thing he had in Danetta. Instead of smiling or being overjoyed about the love that was in his heart, Marshall felt such misery, way down deep in his soul. He ejected the CD and then drove the car into the parking garage.

He met up with Danetta in the ICU. She was standing at the nurses' station, waiting on the nurse to get off the phone. She looked up at Marshall as he walked over to her. "You're staying?"

He nodded, not trusting himself to speak.

The nurse hung up the phone and told Danetta, "Your aunt is still in surgery. It may take a few hours, but when he's finished, the doctor will be out to speak with you."

Danetta sat down in the back of the waiting room. Marshall told her, "I'm going to get us something to eat in the cafeteria. What do you want?"

She waved off the suggestion of food.

"You have to eat, Danetta. We don't know how long we'll be here tonight."

She didn't respond.

"I'll be right back." He headed down to the cafeteria and picked a dinner of mac and cheese, green beans and baked chicken for Danetta and mashed potatoes, gravy and fried chicken for himself. The food didn't look all that appetizing, but at least they would have something in their stomachs.

As he headed back up to the ICU his cell rang. He checked the caller ID and saw that it was Kevin. Answering the phone, he said, "What's up, man?"

"That's what I'm calling to find out. You were pretty teed off when you left the club last night. So, are we cool or what?"

"Yeah, we're cool. I was just in a bad place last night. It had nothing to do with you."

"Are you going to meet me at the gym for our workout in the morning?"

"Wouldn't miss it."

"Have you talked to Danetta about what happened with you and her?"

"Not yet. We're at the hospital right now. Her aunt's in surgery."

"Aw naw. I'm sorry to hear that, man. Give Danetta a hug from me. I know how much her aunt means to her," Kevin said.

"Thanks, Kevin, I'll do that." They hung up just as Marshall walked back into the ICU and handed Danetta a Styrofoam container and said, "Eat."

She opened the Styrofoam container. She loved macaroni and cheese. She glanced over at Marshall's container. He had mashed potatoes and fried chicken. Danetta didn't like fried chicken and Marshall knew it.

He handed her a sixteen-ounce cup. "I got you a soda. I know you keep iced tea at home, but you usually drink Sunkist at work."

He was right. This man sitting next to her knew who she was and what she was about. She had tried everything to get over loving him. But now that her aunt was in surgery fighting for her life, Danetta didn't have the energy to fight Marshall. She realized that she wouldn't have wanted Stan or anyone else to be with her at a time like this. She needed Marshall and that was that.

Marshall saw the look in Danetta's eyes and knew that she was worrying about her aunt. He put his hand over hers. "You know that Aunt Sarah is a strong woman, right?"

Danetta nodded.

"She'll come through this and she'll be strong enough to chase me around another room with an umbrella."

Danetta's eyes bucked. "You remember that?"

"How could I forget it? There I was crashing at your crib, trying to get over a massive hangover, when your aunt busted through your bedroom door and started screaming at me."

"Do you remember what she said?" Danetta asked, with the glint of laughter in her eyes.

"Woman, if you think I could ever forget

something like that, then you don't know me at all. Aunt Sarah was waving around that long umbrella like it was a weapon, saying," his voice went higher as he mimicked Sarah, " 'The works of Satan will not prevail up in this dorm room. Now you get your too-cute-for-your-own-good self on out of here.' "

Danetta was in full-blown laughter now as she doubled over. "I-it took m-me a week to convince her that I had slept on the couch and not in bed with you." As she sat back up, their eyes met and locked.

Marshall felt something pass between them and he knew that this was the moment he'd been waiting for. He blurted out, "I didn't sleep with Marissa."

"Huh? What?"

"Marissa . . . the woman you saw leaving my house this morning."

Danetta turned away from him and began eating her food.

"Okay, I know you don't believe me, but it's the truth. I met Marissa a couple of years ago. And I slept with her, promised to call, but I never did." He shrugged. The truth was all he had right now, no matter how harsh it sounded. "I ran into her again at the last business retreat I went on."

"The one I asked you not to take any

women to," she said as she took a bite of her chicken.

"I didn't hook up with her at the retreat. She was there because she has a business of her own. She saw me there and when I didn't remember her, she reminded me that I had slept with her and then never called, and then she slapped me."

Danetta tried not to smile, but she couldn't help it. The thought of some woman slapping Marshall was too awesome for her to contain her giggles.

"It wasn't funny when it happened. If I wasn't such a gentleman, I would have slapped her back. God knows I wanted to."

Danetta eyed him as he called himself a gentleman.

"Hey, I am a gentleman. Anyway, I ran into Marissa last night when Kevin took me to a nightclub to calm me down . . . I had been so angry because of what happened between you and me that I couldn't relax. I was headed home, then I saw Marissa." He wasn't going to admit that he hadn't known the woman's name. He just couldn't take any more of this laughfest Danetta had going on. "I apologized to her for the way I treated her. I told her that I now knew how she felt."

Danetta stopped laughing. "Wait a minute.

210

Did you tell that woman about what happened with us?"

"I didn't tell her your name. I just told her that I felt hurt by the fact that all you wanted from me was sex . . . and that helped me to see her point of view. Then we left the club and went to my place so that she could tell me about herself. But I swear, all we did was talk."

Now it was Danetta's turn to admit the truth. "Look, Marshall, I thought you wanted me to say that I just wanted sex and nothing more. All you've ever wanted was to date women who understood the no-strings-attached rule."

"I want more now."

Danetta raised her hands, trying to put a halt to the conversation. "Look, none of this is my business. You told me a long time ago that all you wanted was friendship from me. I'm the one who misunderstood what was happening between us yesterday and tried to take it to the next level."

"But that's just it. You didn't misunderstand anything. I did want to be with you."

"You don't have to placate me just because my aunt is sick."

"That's not what I'm doing. If you would just listen to me —"

"I've got a headache, Marshall. I need to

close my eyes for a few minutes, so can we please just stop talking?"

With her eyes closed and her head leaning against the wall, Danetta tried to shut out all the noises around her so that she could process the things Marshall had just said. Was he really trying to get her to believe that he wanted her last night? If that's the case, then why did he run out of her house like Satan was serving ice water in Hades and he had to get in line to quench his thirst?

She drifted off to sleep and met up with the Marshall of her dreams rather than the one seated next to her. Both were scrumptious to look at, but this Marshall adored her above all others. There was no Marissa or Veronica in his vocabulary. The only name coming out of his mouth was Danetta and he was screaming it over and over again . . .

"Danetta, Danetta, wake up." Marshall shook her.

Danetta jumped up as her eyes popped open. She looked around as if trying to get her bearings. "Huh? What?"

Marshall had a devilish grin on his face as he asked, "What were you dreaming about?"

"What? Why?"

"You were moaning."

She smacked him on the shoulder. "Stop lying, Marshall. You just have a dirty mind."

"I know what I heard. And I wish I could have been a fly on the wall of your dreams so I could have gotten my happy on, too."

You didn't have to be a fly on the wall, you were the star of the show, Danetta thought as she attempted to exorcise Marshall from her mind, heart and dreams. She was beginning to think that her misery was of her own making. She had foolishly gone into business with a man that she knew she was infatuated with . . . even though she knew he didn't feel the same way about her. For years, she stood by and watched Marshall go from one relationship to the next, her heart cracking a little more each time.

With her aunt now in bad health and Danetta's emotions spiraling out of control, there was no way she could continue to deal with Marshall and all the drama surrounding him. She turned to her friend, took his hand in hers, looked him in the eye and said, "I need to take a leave of absence."

He hesitated and then asked, "Why do I feel like this is about more than taking care of Aunt Sarah?"

She lowered her head as she tried to find a way to make Marshall understand without throwing herself on the altar of humiliation once again. But before she could respond, someone tapped her on the shoulder. Danetta dropped Marshall's hand and turned to face a man in a light green surgical uniform.

"Are you Danetta Harris?"

"Yes."

The doctor smiled, as he offered her his hand. "I'm Dr. Wakefield."

Danetta and Marshall stood up; as she shook the doctor's hand. "How is my aunt doing?"

"She came through surgery like a trouper."

"Thank you so much," Danetta said. She hugged the doctor and then hugged Marshall.

"I told you Aunt Sarah was going to be all right," Marshall said as he held on to Danetta.

Danetta eased out of his arms and turned back to the doctor. "When can I see her?"

"She's asleep right now, so you may want to wait until she wakes up sometime during the early morning hours."

"All right, then. Is it okay if I spend the night in the waiting room?"

"That's fine. I'll tell the nurses to come and get you when she wakes up."

"Thank you so much," she said before turning back to Marshall, but he was no longer standing next to her. She looked around and saw that Marshall had commandeered two love seats and moved them against the wall on the opposite side of the room to where they had been sitting. She noticed that the love seats were directly in front of the flat-screen TV that hung on the wall. Marshall walked over to the nurses' desk and asked for pillows and blankets.

Danetta walked over to him and said, "Thank you for taking care of that for me. I thought I would have to sit up in that chair all night. I never even noticed those love seats."

"It's not going to be that much more comfortable, but at least we can lie down and watch television."

She heard the *we,* but didn't process it until the nurse came back and handed Marshall four pillows, two sheets and two blankets. Turning to him, she asked, "Are you staying here with me tonight?"

"I know how you feel about hospitals and I don't want you to be here by yourself."

"B-but, it's the weekend. I thought you'd probably be going out with Kevin tonight."

"D, I'm sick of hanging out at nightclubs. That's just not my scene anymore. And anyway, I'd rather be here with you." They walked over to the love seat which didn't appear to have enough cushion to provide a comfortable night's sleep. But Marshall didn't complain. He took off his jacket, spread the sheets over the love seats, and placed two pillows on one side and the other two pillows on the other.

"Climb in," he said as he climbed in on his side of the makeshift bed.

As Danetta got in and Marshall pulled the covers over them, she was reminded of the "When a Man Loves a Woman" song they had been listening to in the car. They weren't out in the rain, but Marshall had sure enough given up all his comfort, just because Danetta wanted to stay at the hospital. She loved him all the more for what he was doing, but what did this say about his feelings for her?

CHAPTER 17

There was a long line of women standing outside of an office building, holding applications in their hands. Danetta looked down and noticed that she had an application in her hand, also. But she wasn't standing in the line. A tall, dark brother came from out of nowhere and began escorting her up to the front door of the office building.

As she passed the women, Danetta became acutely aware that she knew a lot of them. Diane stood in spot number seventy-eight. Danetta had eaten a dozen brownies and a tub of cookies-and-cream ice cream when Marshall had started dating her. Veronica was in spot number sixty-five — five brownies, and Marissa was in sixty-four — two brownies, would have been three, but she had left the box at home when she rushed back to the hospital. As she continued to look at the long line of women,

Danetta realized that many of the women in this line had helped her put on the extra ten pounds she had been saddled with. Because each one of them had dated Marshall.

Where was this man taking her? Why were the women cursing at her as she passed them? When he opened the office door, the curses became louder, and one of the women threw something that banged against the plate glass window. The man pulled the door closed and locked it. "The past doesn't matter," he told her. "Only what's happening now matters, remember that."

"Okay," she agreed, not really understanding what she was agreeing to.

He took her down a long, empty hallway. None of the women who'd been standing outside were inside the building, nor could she hear their taunts anymore. As she continued to wonder why Marshall's ex-women were angry with her, the man opened the door to the interview room. A man sat at the head of the table with his head down, sketching something on a piece of paper.

Danetta gave the man a questioning glance.

"Hand him your application."

Danetta shrugged her shoulders, but

walked farther into the room. When she reached the man who appeared to be doodling hearts on a piece of paper rather than working, she handed him her application.

He looked up, and took Danetta's breath away. It was Marshall. As she looked at the paper full of hearts again, she realized that he had written the words, 'Marshall and Danetta forever' in each one of the hearts.

"I don't understand," she said.

He stood up, pulled her into his arms and kissed her with all the passion he'd had bottled up inside since the day they met.

"You're moaning again," Marshall whispered into her ear.

A sweet sensation moved through her and she wanted to cry for the joy of having him so close. She put her arms around him and began moaning in real time.

Marshall shook her. "Danetta, baby, wake up."

Her eyes popped open. She looked around. She wasn't in an office building having her application accepted by Marshall. She was in the hospital, surrounded by other family members who were waiting for news of their loved ones. And she had her arms around Marshall. She removed her arms and sat up. Too embarrassed to look his way, Danetta threw back the covers, got out of their makeshift bed and moved her love seat back against the wall.

He sat up and folded the cover. "Do you want to go see if Aunt Sarah is up yet?"

She looked at the clock on the wall. It was six in the morning. "I think that's a good idea."

They walked over to the nurses' station and asked to be buzzed into the ICU. The nurse unlocked the ICU doors and Marshall and Danetta walked through. Once they were in Sarah's room, Danetta quickly discovered that her aunt was still in a deep sleep. She went to the nurses' station inside the ICU and asked to speak with her aunt's nurse.

A woman in a multicolored smock stepped over to Danetta and said, "Hi, I'm Latonya Matthews and I've been on duty all night, taking care of your aunt."

"Did she wake up anytime during the night?"

Latonya averted her eyes. "No, she didn't."

"Thank you for the information." Danetta turned and hurriedly went back into her aunt's room. She didn't want to ask any more questions for fear that she might learn more than she wanted to know. Marshall was standing by her aunt's bed looking down at her with sorrowful eyes. At that moment, Danetta realized that Marshall truly cared about Aunt Sarah.

He looked up as Danetta entered the room. "She looks so frail. She needs to hurry and wake up and rebuke me about something else I've done that she doesn't approve of."

"Yeah, I'd take a good ol' rebuke from her myself, right now."

Latonya walked into the room. She glanced at the still form of her patient and then turned to Danetta and said, "The doctor wanted me to ask if your aunt has a living will."

Not this again. Once a person got sick, these so-called healers were always trying to find a way to let them die. They'd harassed her mother every single day of that month they stayed in this hospital, constantly coming in the room, telling just how sick she was and taking all her hope away. After they'd taken her hope, they then started telling her that resuscitating her mother would probably do more harm than good . . . and why keep a dying person on a ventilator . . . better to just let her die gracefully. Forget that.

When Danetta didn't answer, Latonya said, "We're only asking because we need to know if we are supposed to resuscitate your

221

aunt if she should stop breathing."

Danetta had been seventeen when they started on this stuff with her mom. At that time, she thought that the doctors were there to do what was best for her mom, and she was too young and too afraid to anger them, to ask them to stop what they were doing. But the buck stopped here, and she was about to let them have it. Walking toward the nurse, she said, "Let me explain something to you so that you never have to ask me again." Danetta's voice began rising with each word. "If Sarah Davis stops breathing, then you had better get every machine known to man in this room and revive her. If she needs to be on a ventilator for a month, then you and everybody in this hospital better hope that nobody unplugs it by mistake . . . because if anything happens to this woman," she said as she pointed at Sarah, "I will sue you, her doctor and this hospital for everything any of you ever thought about owning."

"Danetta, what's wrong?" Marshall came up behind her and pulled her out of Nurse Latonya's face.

"Nothing's wrong," she said to Marshall while still looking at Latonya in a threatening manner.

"You were screaming at the nurse. Something is wrong."

"I'm just letting this nurse and this hospital know where I stand," she said to Marshall, then to Latonya she asked, "You got me . . . I just gave you all the living-will information you need, right?"

The woman nodded and then walked out of the room.

Marshall turned Danetta to face him. He lifted her chin so that she was looking him in the eye. "Don't tell me that nothing is wrong. I have never seen you so upset. That nurse didn't do anything to you, so what am I missing?"

Tears bubbled in her eyes as she put her hand to her face.

He pulled her hand down. She lowered her face. "Look at me, Danetta. I can't fix something that I don't know about."

"You can't fix me, Marshall. I'm all messed up. My aunt is right. This hospital is my fiery furnace."

"Your fiery what?"

"Never mind." She stepped away from him, needing a little breathing room so she could think clearly. "Look, I'm sorry about the way I just acted. When she asked me that question, I just flashed back to the way my mother was treated at this hospital. It was like they killed her with their words . . .

took all her hope away. I can't let them do that to Aunt Sarah."

He took his cell phone out of his pocket and started punching in numbers.

"Who are you calling this early in the morning?"

"Kevin. I'm supposed to meet him at the gym this morning. I'm just calling to cancel."

Danetta took the phone away from him and hit the end button. She handed the phone back to him and said, "Go to the gym, Marshall." She didn't want to need him to stay — couldn't afford to depend on him and then be let down.

"You need me here. I can work out another time."

"No. I won't let you babysit me all day, just because you think I'm a basket case. I will be fine. Go and enjoy your day."

"I can't just leave you here by yourself."

"By myself?" Danetta walked over to the bed and looked at her aunt. Tears fell down her face as she said, "I'm with Aunt Sarah. She'll keep me company." She turned back to Marshall. "So get on out of here, Marshall Windham."

He hesitated before he spoke. "Okay, but I'll be back."

She didn't say anything, just smiled at him.

"I mean it, Danetta. I have a lunch appointment with a potential client, but I'll be back right after that meeting."

Danetta sat down in a chair next to the bed and then grabbed hold of her aunt's hand. She held on to it as if she was pumping life into her aunt.

It pained Marshall to leave Danetta in that hospital, holding on to her aunt like a life preserver. But she was a grown woman, and he had to let her handle her business. So, now he was lifting weights with his boy, Kevin, pretending that he didn't want to run back to Danetta.

"How's your girl doing?"

"She's hurting, man. I was really worried about leaving her at the hospital."

"So, why did you?"

"I think I was kinda crowding her. So I'm letting her handle her business. You know . . . no big deal."

Kevin put the barbells down and laughed. "Dawg, you should see your face. You can't wait to run back to that hospital. You've got it bad."

"Oh shut up and mind your business."

Kevin got off the bench. "Okay, you can

deny all you want. We both know the truth."

Marshall took Kevin's place and bench-pressed two hundred. "Add some more weight."

Kevin ignored the weight request. "Did you talk about what happened between you two the night before last?"

"I told her that I wanted to be with her, but she didn't want to talk about it. I got the impression that she didn't believe me."

"Why don't you just go on and tell her that you're in love with her?"

"What?" Marshall sat up, almost bumping his head on the barbells. He sat there for a moment as Kevin's words drifted into his heart, mind and soul. He loved Danetta. Well yeah, he'd loved her for as long as they'd been friends. But what he was feeling now was different . . . it was not so much that he loved her, but that he was *in* love with her. How and when it had happened, Marshall didn't know, but he knew one thing for sure: Kevin was right, and the very thought of this wondrous thing caused Marshall to laugh out loud.

"What's so funny?"

With a look of astonishment on his face, Marshall confessed, "Out of all the women I've dated, I'm in love with the one I never slept with."

"Boy, shut your mouth." Kevin glanced around hoping that none of the women were listening. "If women hear talk like that, they might start putting the goodies on lock."

"That's your problem, man. I apparently am off the market."

Kevin couldn't wait to bust his bubble. "Last I heard, Danetta wasn't interested in no love connection with you . . . just a slam, bam, thank you, Mr. Windham."

"That's what you think." He stood and gave Kevin a direct stare. "I'm not about to let Danetta or any other woman use me like some plaything. Danetta will come around, because from this moment forward, it's either all or nothing."

CHAPTER 18

It had been two hours since Marshall had left her at the hospital. Danetta was about to pull her hair out as she sat and watched her aunt remain in a deep sleep. At about ten that morning, Ryla and Surry stopped by to check on her. Danetta sat in the ICU waiting area with her friends. "Thank you for coming out here this morning. I really appreciate it."

"You know you don't have to thank us. We want to be here. How is your aunt?" Surry asked.

"About the same. We're waiting for her to wake up, so the doctor can determine her prognosis for recovery."

"You look like you climbed the walls all night. You need to try to get some sleep," Ryla told her.

Danetta rubbed her eyes. "Truth be told, I'm so tired, I could probably sleep for three days. But the chairs in this waiting area are terrible. When Marshall and I woke up this morning, we were so sore it didn't make sense."

"Wait a minute," Ryla said, holding up her hand. "Back up and rewind. Did you just say that Marshall spent the night at the hospital with you?"

"Yeah, we slept on those love seats over there." Danetta pointed to the left of where they were sitting.

"I can't picture Mr. Kool Mo Dee, pretty boy, Marshall Windham getting kinks in his back to lay up in a hospital waiting room, when he knew he wouldn't be getting nothing for his effort," Surry said. Then she had a thought and turned to Danetta with horror in her eyes. "Please tell me that you didn't have sex with that man in a hospital waiting room?"

"Of course I didn't. Do you think I'm nuts or something?" Danetta shook her head at her friend's antics. "Marshall stayed because he knew that I was terrified of being in this particular hospital, because my mom died here years ago."

"Oh, well then that was nice of him," Surry said while looking guilty for having such a dirty mind.

"I'm proud of Marshall; that brother is finally growing up. Now if I could only get

Mr. Noel Carter to join the land of grown-ups."

"I wasn't aware that you'd had any contact with Jaylen's father," Danetta said.

"I haven't. The problem is that Jaylen keeps asking about her father. Her classmates are always talking about their fathers and now that Jaylen is seven, she's started asking more questions about Noel."

"Okay, what's so wrong with that? Why don't you just tell the man that he has a daughter and give Jaylen what she wants and deserves . . . a father?" Surry asked.

"It's not that simple, Surry."

"Sure it is. You just call the man up and tell him that he has a seven-year-old child."

"Noel is running for Congress now, and I just think that receiving news like this now would just complicate his life at a time when he needs to be focused on his campaign."

"Don't you think he would still want to know?" Danetta asked.

Ryla lowered her head in shame. "Well, considering that I never even told Noel that I was pregnant when I left, I just don't know how he's going to react when he finds out what I did."

"I'm sorry, Ryla, you're my girl and all. But what you did was foul.com," Surry said, taking a phrase from her favorite personality on *The Braxton's Family Values.*

"And I thought I had problems with trying to figure out what's going on inside Marshall's head . . . As David Letterman says, I wouldn't give your troubles to a monkey on a rock." Danetta and her friends continued to laugh and talk for a few more minutes. Then she went back in to sit with her aunt.

By noon, when her aunt still hadn't opened her eyes, Danetta caught the grim expressions on the nurses' and doctors' faces as they came in and out of the room. They wouldn't say anything to her, though. Danetta was at least grateful for that. No one was trying to give her a jolt of reality at a time when she needed to cling to as much faith as possible.

The doctors couldn't help, her aunt couldn't help herself and Danetta was powerless to do anything at all. But then, like a mighty river, her aunt's words rushed back into Danetta's heart and mind. There was someone who could help. He was the only one she could turn to. It was someone she had turned her back on long ago in this very place. His name was Jesus . . . and Danetta was determined to find him and plead her case.

She stood up, kissed her aunt on the

forehead and then told her, "All right, Aunt Sarah, I'm about to jump in this fiery furnace with both feet." She then walked out of her aunt's room and down to the hospital chapel. As Danetta walked in she was stunned to see that not much had changed in the room since she'd last seen it, over a decade ago. Even the wooden benches looked the same.

As she walked to the front of the chapel, to the very front pew, the one that she'd sat on all those years ago, Danetta felt panic trying to overtake her. She stopped walking and took in slow, deep breaths . . . inhale . . . exhale. She made her way to the seat, but before sitting and handling her business, she looked down at the spot that she had claimed when she had been an impressionable child and her mind's eye took her back to those painful days.

One night the temperature in her mother's room had dropped to freezing. Danetta had requested extra blankets from the nurse. She had not only covered up, but had buried her head as well and she'd still ended up with a cold by morning. Her mother, on the other hand, hadn't even used the extra covers that had been given to her. When she'd asked her mother why she hadn't used the extra covers, her mother had said, "I wasn't cold."

The nurse had given Danetta one of her I-pity-you looks and at that moment, Danetta knew that her mother's body had gone numb and she no longer registered the difference between hot and cold. Danetta had rushed down to the chapel and prayed, begging God to turn their situation around . . . restore her mother's body to health.

But then the next night her mother needed a blood transfusion because her body was no longer reproducing the blood it needed to survive on its own. Danetta had known that the blood transfusion was a sign from God. How many times had she read in the Bible about the power being in the blood? She'd run down to the chapel and prayed that night also, confident that God was working a miracle out for them. The last week her mother was in the hospital, she'd come to the chapel several times a day. She'd prayed and prayed, begging God to hear her cries.

Then her mother slipped into a coma and the last prayer that Danetta prayed there or anywhere else was when she begged God to take her mom on to heaven and put her out of her misery. It seemed like all of her other prayers had fallen on deaf ears, but God chose to hear that particular one. The next day, her sweet mother quietly passed away. Danetta had never been able to forgive God for answering that prayer. She'd never admitted that to anyone, but as she sat back in her familiar seat, she now admitted it to God.

Tears streamed down her face as she looked at the cross of Jesus hanging on the wall and said, "I thought my aunt had been a fool to believe in You . . . the God who answers the wrong prayers. I hadn't been ready for my mom to leave me. I told you as much. But You didn't listen. You only chose to hear my unselfish prayer . . . when I couldn't take my mom's suffering anymore and then begged You to take her home with You. But I had wanted You to hear all the other prayers I'd prayed to You first."

She sighed and wiped some of the tears from her face. "Now You've had my mom with You for thirteen years. I don't understand people who say I'm supposed to *count it all joy* because none of this has been joyful for me.

"But the truth of the matter is that I had truly loved You once, and I trusted You. I want to be that person again. But I need You to give me my faith back. Can You do that for me?"

She stood up and walked to the altar in front of the cross, and got on her knees. She lifted her head heavenward and raised her hands as she made a bargain with God. "Wake up my aunt, Lord Jesus, restore my faith and I will serve You until the day I die."

She lowered her head as a soft wind blew into the windowless room. And as she closed her eyes, Danetta could swear that she smelled the flowery fragrance of her mother's favorite perfume, as she felt loving arms wrap themselves around her.

"I've missed you," Danetta said to her mom as she lay down on the floor and allowed the loving feeling to envelop her. She continued to cry out to God on her aunt's behalf. After about an hour, Danetta's faith had increased to the point that she jumped up and ran back upstairs to her aunt's room. She had a feeling that Aunt Sarah was awake and waiting for her to visit. But when she got to her aunt's room, the smile that had been on Danetta's face all the way through the hospital corridors fell. She had a momentary lapse of faith, but then she remembered a Bible verse she'd read as a child: "Faith is the substance of things hoped for, the evidence of things not seen."

She wasn't tucking tail and giving in this time. Danetta wasn't about to pray any more prayers of release. Her aunt was waking up today and that was all there was to it. She walked over to Aunt Sarah's bed and told her, "Look, Aunt Sarah, I don't know what you think you're doing sleeping the day away. But I've got news for you. I just made a bargain with God. I told Him that if you wake up, I will attend church with you again."

There was no reaction on her aunt's face to that particular bit of news, but Danetta thundered on anyway. "So, if you want me to live up to my bargain with God, I suggest that you wake up and make me."

"When she wakes up, I'll take both of you to church."

Danetta swung around. Marshall was standing in the doorway looking just as fine as he always did. Danetta knew she looked a wreck. But he was looking at her as if she fulfilled all of his desires. She ran her hands through her hair as she said, "I didn't expect you back so soon."

He rushed to her and pulled her into his arms. "Aw, baby, you look like you've been through the wringer today. I shouldn't have left you."

It felt so good being in his arms that she nearly forgot that she was in a hospital and that her aunt was lying in the bed next to them fighting for her life. For a slim moment in time, all her thoughts centered around this man, and when he pulled away a bit and looked down at her, Danetta saw the heat of desire in his eyes and she could do nothing to stop herself from begging him to kiss her right then and there.

He lowered his lips and explored her mouth like a scuba diver searching for her hidden treasure. They connected on a level that was more than physical, more than emotional . . . it was spiritual. Their love would stand the test of time, because it was founded on so much more than mere sexual attraction. They had respect and love for one another.

When their lips parted, Danetta said, "Wow, that was some hello."

He smiled down at her. "You haven't seen anything yet, baby. I really go to town when I'm saying good night."

CHAPTER 19

"Come on, let's go get something to eat."

Danetta looked at the still form of her aunt and shook her head. "I don't want to leave her right now."

"Have you eaten anything since last night?" Marshall asked.

"No."

"And you barely ate any of that food either."

"Hospital food isn't all that appetizing," she admitted.

"Nevertheless, you'll be of no use to Aunt Sarah if you don't keep your strength up." He grabbed her hand and began moving her out of the room. "I'll ask the nurse to call us if anything changes, but I'm taking you downstairs right now to get something to eat."

She saluted him as if he were a sergeant in the United States Army. "Yes, sir, Mr. Windham, sir."

"Keep talking like that, baby. I like it when my women are submissive."

She shoved him.

Marshall laughed and then he gave the nurse his and Danetta's cell phone numbers and told her that they would be down in the cafeteria for a little while. They walked hand in hand to the cafeteria. Marshall paid for their food and then they sat down at one of the round tables. It might have only been cafeteria food, but Danetta ate like the food had come from Cheesecake Factory, one of her favorite casual restaurants.

"See, I knew you were hungry," Marshall said as Danetta cleaned the meat off the bone of a piece of barbecue chicken.

"Hungry is not the word. I guess I spent so much time in the chapel praying today, that I didn't realize how hungry I was. Hopefully God will see my starvation as a sacrifice to Him and be more inclined to wake up Aunt Sarah."

Marshall smiled. "I've never heard you talk about God or praying much. You used to tell me that it made no sense to pray, when a person could just put in the effort and get everything he or she wanted, instead of waiting for it to fall out of the sky."

She winced at her words. But there was nothing she could do about the past, because she truly had felt that way. "My aunt told me that I lost my faith while in this hospital. She believes that her illness is going to help me get it back. I just hope that she's right, because if she doesn't wake up . . ." She left the rest unsaid.

"Well, you don't have anything to worry about, because I've been praying for Aunt Sarah to wake up, also." Teasingly he added, "You might be too much of a heathen for God to listen to your prayers, but I got this."

"Yeah, if I'm a heathen, then what are you?"

"Woman, don't sit here questioning me about crazy stuff. You need to finish your food so we can get back upstairs."

"Mmph, whatever."

They finished their food and then headed back upstairs. Marshall joined Danetta's hand with his again. Danetta felt as if she were in an alternate universe. One in which she belonged to Marshall and he belonged to her. But how had this happened and when would she wake up? "I don't understand you at all," she said as they headed to the elevator.

"I'm not that complicated."

"Who are you trying to kid, Marshall Windham? You are the most complicated man I know. Like this for example." She

240

lifted their hands up high; he was still holding on to her hand. "You're walking through this hospital holding hands with me; you kissed me in my aunt's hospital room. I just don't know what to make of your actions."

There was a darkened alcove off to the side of the cafeteria. Marshall pulled Danetta over there and with her back pressed against the wall and him standing so close she could hardly breathe, he told her, "For some reason you don't seem to believe that I want to be with you. But that's the truth. I don't know how long it will take for me to convince you of that, but I'm not going anywhere . . . Oh, and I need you to delete your online profile."

"Why?" She wasn't about to admit that she'd already asked Ryla to delete it for her.

"Because, I'm not about to watch my woman go on dates with other men. That's just not happening."

Her heart exploded with joy at his words, but she still didn't understand him. "Why, Marshall? Why do you want me now, but not back when we were in college?"

He put his hand under her chin and gently touched his lips to hers. The kiss was quick, but soft and it spoke of hope and promise. When they broke apart and she was looking into his eyes, he said, "I know you were

241

upset that I turned you down in college. But I'm not."

She stepped back, trying to break the trance that such close contact was putting her in. Folding her arms, she said, "If you're not the least bit remorseful about the way you treated me back then, why should I want anything to do with you now?"

He grabbed her arm, pulling her back to him. "Hear me out, baby. Give me a minute to explain."

She rolled her eyes.

He ignored her attitude and continued, "If I had been with you back in college, we wouldn't be friends right now. I know that, and I also had sense enough to realize that our friendship was too important to throw away for the sake of a bad relationship."

"You don't know that," Danetta protested. "You never even gave me a chance. If you had, we probably would be married by now with three kids —"

"And a divorce," he said, interrupting the dream she'd carried in her heart all these years. "Look, Danetta, we both know that I don't have a good track record for maintaining friendships with my sex partners. If they aren't slapping me or slitting my tires, they usually try to avoid me all together . . . and I try my best to avoid them as well."

A tear trickled down Danetta's face; Marshall wiped it away.

"It wouldn't have been like that with us," she said, confidently.

"It would have, baby. Don't you see? It has never been a question of whether you were good enough for me . . . but I needed to be the kind of man who could give you the love you deserved. And even though I knew I couldn't, I still couldn't bear living without you. That's the reason I asked you to join me as a partner in Windham Enterprises. It gave me an excuse to be with you."

Danetta smirked. "Oh really? And all this time, I thought we became partners because you had the money, but I had the brains."

He laughed as he kissed her on the forehead. "You do have the brains, Danetta. Brains and beauty. And I don't want to waste another day without having you completely in my life."

Skeptically, she asked, "How do I know that this isn't just a ploy of yours? I've seen the way you've been looking at me lately."

"Baby, I'm not even gon' lie and act like I haven't noticed how sexy you are. But let's be real . . . you were trying to put it on me the other night, so if all I wanted was to hit it, I could have done that then."

She hit his shoulder, embarrassed that he

would remind her of her wanton behavior. "You just lost two cool points for that one."

Marshall put her hands in his. "Point-blank, what I'm trying to tell you is . . . I can't get you off my mind. At first I thought I was just going through a midlife crisis or something, but now I know different." He looked into her eyes, praying that she could see everything he was feeling. "Sometimes, I think I love you more than I love myself, and I'm just praying that you feel for me even an ounce of the love I feel for you."

Tears streamed down Danetta's face as she took in every word Marshall said to her. And it was at that moment that she knew she would be able to trust Marshall, he wouldn't trample on her heart as he'd done for so many years with all those women he'd dated. Marshall's heart now belonged to her, and nothing else mattered. She put her arms around his neck. "I've been trying to talk myself out of loving you for so long."

"Has it worked?"

In answer she kissed him with all the passion she'd stored up for years, waiting for him to give her a chance. Just as his hands began to travel, Danetta's cell phone rang. She continued kissing Marshall, not wanting to break the spell. But as the phone kept ringing, she remembered that she was in a hospital and a nurse might be calling her about her aunt. Pulling her lips away from Marshall's, she took the phone out of her jacket pocket and hit the talk button.

"Miss Harris, is that you?" a voice on the other end asked.

"This is Danetta Harris, how may I help you?"

"You might want to come back upstairs. Someone has been asking for you ever since she woke up."

Danetta relayed the message to Marshall. They then ran for the elevator and impatiently waited for its arrival. They touched, hugged and kissed all the way to the ICU floor. Once the elevator released them, they ran all the way back to Sarah's room. And then Danetta witnessed the most beautiful thing she'd ever seen in her life. Aunt Sarah was sitting up in bed, sipping water as the nurse held the cup for her.

The nurse set the cup on the tray table and Danetta ran to her aunt and threw her arms around the woman's neck and cried out, "Thank you, Lord . . . thank you." When she released her aunt and looked at her, she said, "I can't believe this."

"Why can't you believe it?" Aunt Sarah asked, "It's what you prayed for, right?"

As tears streamed down her face, Danetta

didn't trust her voice to answer, so she just nodded.

Sarah turned to Marshall and asked, "So, when are we going to church?"

In answer, Marshall asked a question of his own, "How about a church wedding?"

Danetta's mouth dropped open. She swerved around to face him. "What did you say?"

Marshall swaggered over to his woman, lifted her hands and kissed the backs of each one. Then with a teasing glint in his eye, he said, "You know, considering you are the brains of our operation, it sure does take you a while to catch on."

She could barely breathe as she asked, "What do you mean?"

"When I said I want to be with you, I didn't just mean for a night, a week or a month. This thing with us is forever, baby. I want to marry you. So, what do you say?"

What does a woman say when her dream is standing before her, asking her to step into reality and live in it with him? "Yes, Marshall, thanks for making my dreams come true."

CHAPTER 20

As far as Marshall was concerned, the dream had just begun. He'd kept his promise and taken Danetta and Aunt Sarah to church in mid-March, the week after she was released from the hospital. The three of them thoroughly enjoyed themselves during praise and worship. Marshall even found himself taking notes during the pastor's sermon.

Danetta leaned over and whispered to him, "It feels like coming home."

He smiled; his baby was happy, so it was all good with him, as well. "Then we need to keep on coming . . . I never want to forget where home is."

"Thank you for being okay with this," she said and then turned back to the pastor to finish listening to the sermon.

Marshall knew that Danetta wasn't thanking him for being okay with attending church, but about the conversation they'd had the night he'd given her the engagement ring. And in truth, as he thought back on their conversation, Marshall still wasn't sure if he was totally okay with what he'd agreed to.

He'd gone to the jewelers and picked out a three-carat emerald-cut diamond ring. He then picked up Danetta from the hospital and took her to McCormick & Schmick's. He couldn't wait to give her the ring he'd picked out. The previous night at the hospital, he'd blurted out that he wanted to marry her, but he was unprepared and wished that he had waited until he was able to hand her a ring. But he was going to make up for that tonight.

Danetta sat down and nervously looked around. "I don't know if I like having our first date in the same place I was accused of being a man-stealer."

"This isn't our first date," he said as he sat down across from her.

Danetta laughed. "Don't even try to claim all of our business dinners as dates, because I'm not going for that."

"Don't you remember our dance at that nice little restaurant I took you to? I certainly wasn't thinking about business then and I hope you weren't either."

She blushed a bit, remembering the restaurant and how she had felt being with him that night.

"And anyway," Marshall continued, "I brought you back to McCormick's because this is the place we shared our first kiss." He leaned over and touched his lips to hers.

"Oh yeah, that's right. We did kiss in this restaurant." He kissed her again and she said, "I'm liking this place better and better with each kiss."

They ordered dinner. This time Danetta was even able to eat her meal without some woman showing up at the table and demanding that she give Marshall back. By the time the dessert arrived, Danetta was counting her blessings just for being able to have a man that didn't belong to anyone else. But Marshall went and topped everything off by getting down on one knee and handing her the most beautiful ring she had ever seen.

"Baby, when I asked you to marry me, it was in the heat of the moment so I didn't do it right." A waiter walked to the table carrying two dozen red roses and two glasses filled with champagne. He set the items on the table and left as quickly as he'd arrived. Marshall continued, "I trust you're okay with receiving these roses from me?"

She nodded, not trusting that her voice

wouldn't crack as she tried to speak.

He put her hand in his and said, "I don't just want to be business partners anymore. I want to be with you for the rest of my life. Will you please marry me, Danetta?"

Without hesitation she said, "Yes!" He put the ring on her finger and then their lips joined again, while thunderous applause erupted around them.

As the applause died down, Marshall whispered in his woman's ear, "I want you to come home with me tonight. I think we need to finish what we started the other night, don't you?"

"About that," Danetta said with a look on her face that told Marshall he was not about to like what she had to say next.

"About what?" he asked as he sat back down in his seat and focused on her. She nervously played with her napkin until he took it out of her hand. "Talk to me, baby. What's on your mind?"

"Well, I really hate disappointing you," she said slowly. "But I think you were right about us not having sex the other night, and I'd like to wait until after we're married."

He had begun sipping his champagne, but with Danetta's final words, the liquid sputtered out of his mouth as he asked, "Is this a joke?"

She shook her head.

"I don't understand what's going on, Danetta. Are you still trying to pay me back for the other night? Because if so, it's not necessary. You've won, baby. I want you and only you and I want to show you, tonight."

She put her hand in his and squeezed. "I used to think that the only problem I had with you was that I couldn't trust you with my heart. But this thing with my aunt helped me to see that you were never the real issue. No matter what you would have done, I still wouldn't have been able to trust you or anyone else, because I had lost my faith in God. Now that I've got it back, I want to do this thing right."

"We are doing it right, baby; I just put a ring on your finger," he explained.

"I want our union to be blessed by God. So, I'm hoping and praying that you will come into agreement with me on not making love until we get married."

"We must be leaving for Las Vegas in the morning; is that what you have planned?"

"No, silly, I want a real wedding."

"And I want to be with my woman, so we need to find a compromise in here somewhere," Marshall stated.

The compromise came in the form of a

short engagement. Marshall and Danetta said their vows three months after getting engaged. Marshall had threatened to go to the justice of the peace every day of those three months. So, needless to say, Marshall rushed through his vows, kissed his bride and then walked her to the back of the sanctuary for the receiving line. Once they had shaken all the guests' hands, Marshall handed Danetta's bouquet to Aunt Sarah and whispered in the woman's ear, "We'll see you later."

Sarah looked up at her new nephew and smiled. "Don't you get yourself lost, boy."

He had a devilish grin on his face as he grabbed Danetta's arm and escorted her to their waiting limo.

"That boy is up to something," Aunt Sarah said as she made sure the guests had directions to the reception hall.

Inside the limo, Marshall opened a bottle of champagne and poured the liquid into two glasses. He passed one to Danetta, who was not a drinker, but it was her wedding day. She took the glass from her husband and said, "Thank you, Mr. Windham."

"You're welcome, Mrs. Windham." He held up his glass in a toast and said, "To us."

"To us, indeed, baby," she said as she

drank the intoxicating liquid. Then she noticed that the driver turned left when he needed to turn right for the reception hall. She tapped on the window.

Marshall pulled her back. "What's wrong?"

"He's going the wrong way."

"No, he's not. I told him to take us home first."

Home for Danetta beginning today was Marshall's house. It was the bigger of the two, so they had agreed that she would move in after the wedding. "Home? Marshall, we don't have time to go home."

"Relax, baby, your man has this covered."

She leaned back in her seat and sipped from her glass, wondering what craziness Marshall was trying to pull. She didn't have long to wait. When Harry, the chauffeur, pulled up to their house, he opened Danetta's door and she got out and stood on the lawn, smiling as she looked at the sign that hung above the door, which said, 'Welcome Home, Mrs. Windham'.

Marshall got out of the car and walked over to her. She turned to him and asked, "Is that what you wanted me to see?"

Marshall picked her up like a man who'd eaten all his spinach and walked her to the front door. "No, baby, what I want you to see is inside."

Laughing, Danetta yelled back to Harry, "Don't leave us. We'll only be a minute."

"That's what you think," Marshall said as he pushed the door open, carried Danetta over the threshold and then put her down in the foyer.

"Marshall, quit playing. We have over two hundred guests waiting for us at the reception hall."

"Baby, your man has been waiting, too. You've got the ring, so now it's time to sing for daddy."

She backed away from him, giggling, but still trying to get away. "You are such a baby, you've only been waiting three months, Marshall."

He menacingly followed her, backing her toward the direction he wanted her to go. "Try ten years, dear wife. I've waited ten years for you, and I'm not about to wait a minute longer."

She backed into the stairs. She turned and noticed that a trail of rose petals were scattered all over the stairway. Astonishment written all over her face, she turned back to Marshall. "What did you do?"

"Follow the trail and find out."

"Do I hear music?"

He didn't answer.

Curiosity got the better of her and she began climbing the stairs. The trail of rose petals continued at the top of the stairs. The music was louder now; it was a soft, seductive instrumental that was causing Danetta to think about more important things than a reception hall full of guests. She followed the trail to Marshall's bedroom which, of course, was now their bedroom.

She put her hand on the doorknob and he put his hand on her zipper. As she opened the door, he unzipped her dress. "Stop that." She swatted his hands as she scurried away from him.

He closed the door. "Nowhere to run now, baby."

She stood on the opposite side of the bed and looked around the room. The lights were off, the shades drawn. Fragrant candles were lit all around the room. The rose petals were piled together in the shape of hearts all over the floor and on the king-size bed that she would be sharing with Marshall. "How did you have time to do all of this?"

"I had a wedding to attend today, so I couldn't do all of this on my own. I hired a service because I didn't want the candles to be lit until we were on our way home."

"Smart thinking." She was swooning over his thoughtfulness, but she had to pull herself together. There was no way she could let him get away with this. "But we have to go, Marshall, our guests won't even be able to eat until we get there."

"Oh, they'll eat, don't worry about them." He swaggered toward her, with the look of desire in his eyes, she couldn't turn away from him. He grabbed her hands and pulled her onto the bed with him. "Come on, Mrs. Windham, I told you I wanted to show you something."

She pulled back, laughter in her eyes now. "But wait a minute, Mr. Windham. If I get in that bed with you, what does this mean for us? Do you want a relationship with me? Do you want to marry me?"

"I want it all, baby. I want it all."

Back at the reception hall, Aunt Sarah was wringing her hands with worry. Kevin approached her and asked, "What's wrong, Mrs. Davis?"

"I can't reach Marshall or Danetta. They aren't answering their cell phones and they should have been here by now."

Kevin grinned. "Oh, they'll be here. But it will probably be a while. You might want to let the people eat."

Sarah grabbed Kevin's arm and pulled him to the side. "Spill it right now, young man. What do you know?"

Kevin raised his hands in surrender. "No disrespect, Mrs. Harris, because you raised your niece right. But you can't keep a man waiting for three months and not expect him to pull an abduction."

"He did what?"

Kevin's grin got wider. "Like I said, you might want to go ahead and serve the dinner."

She popped Kevin on the back of his head for grinning like a fool. "Okay, you get the microphone and discreetly let the guests know that we are going to start the reception before the bride and groom get here. And I'll get the hostess ready to serve the food."

Kevin walked over to the band and asked to borrow the microphone for a moment. He then turned to the crowd and said. "Ah, yo, everybody. My boy, Marshall, is handling his business right now, so if we make y'all wait to eat until he lets Danetta out the house, you just might starve to death up in here." Kevin laughed his head off and nudged one of the band members and then added, like he was giving the punch line of an inside joke, "I'm just sayin', you know what I mean."

Aunt Sarah ran over and snatched the microphone out of his hands. "I wish you would have told me that you didn't have good sense," she said as she slapped him upside the back of his head again.

They were in the limo headed to the reception hall, two hours later. Danetta's hair was loose and her makeup needed to be retouched, but she didn't care. She leaned back into her husband's loving arms. "Now I see why you were so adamant about us taking our wedding photos before the wedding."

The grin on his face was that of a man well satisfied. "Yeah baby, I put my plan in motion a month ago."

"Well, I'm glad you're happy, because I am going to be totally embarrassed when I face the people we've kept waiting. You know they know why."

They pulled up at the reception hall and as they got out of the limo, Danetta noticed Ryla and Jaylen sprinting toward the parking lot. "Ryla," Danetta called after her friend.

Ryla turned, and saw Danetta. She handed Jaylen the keys to the car and then walked back toward her friend. They hugged. "Hey girl, showed up in time to cut the cake, huh?"

"Yeah, something like that." Then she asked her friend, "Why are you leaving? Stay and enjoy the rest of the evening with us."

Ryla leaned over and whispered in Danetta's ear, "Noel is in there. He saw Jaylen, and I think he figured out what I did. I've got to go."

With a worried look on her face, Danetta told Ryla, "Okay, girl, I'll call you next week to see how you're doing." She turned to Marshall.

"What's wrong, baby?" he asked. "Are you still nervous about facing our guests?"

Danetta turned to her husband. He was everything she ever wanted and so much more. This was her good thing; what did she care if a couple of hundred people knew what she and her husband had been doing. "You know what, Mr. Windham? We don't even have to go in there. Come on, let's go back home."

"But, baby, I really want a piece of that cake," Marshall cajoled.

She rolled her eyes heavenward. What was she going to do with this man? One thing was for sure, she wasn't throwing him back. So, she might as well just hang with her husband . . . enjoy the cake and enjoy the party. Then later on tonight, she would enjoy her man again . . . and again.

ABOUT THE AUTHOR

Vanessa Miller is a bestselling author, playwright and motivational speaker. She started writing as a child, spending countless hours either reading or writing poetry, short stories, stage plays and novels. Vanessa's creative endeavors took on new meaning in 1994 when she became a Christian. Since then, her writing has been centered on themes of redemption, often focusing on characters facing multidimensional struggles.

Vanessa's novels have received rave reviews, with several appearing on *Essence* magazine's bestseller list. Her work has received numerous awards, including Best Christian Fiction Mahogany Award and a Red Rose Award for Excellence in Christian Fiction. Miller graduated from Capital University with a degree in organizational communication. She is an ordained minister in her church, explaining, "God has called me to minister to readers and to help them rediscover their place with the Lord."

She is currently working on a trilogy, For Your Love, for Harlequin Kimani Romance. *Her Good Thing* is the first book in the trilogy. She is also working on a historical set in the Gospel Era for Abingdon Press. Her first book in the Gospel Series, *How Sweet the Sound,* releases in 2013.